Ch

An Anthology of Moseley Writers

Edited by

David Croser, Chris Randall, Elizabeth Tunstall & Faith Walsh

Changes © 2020

Moseley Writers Group

Breakfast in Moseley © Jan Inglis

Morta © Kathryn Cooper

Rebirth © Evelyn Kemp

Document 18 © Andrew Brazier

The Forever Home © Sarah Bartlett

Perso e Trovato © SL Jones

Osaka Nights © Sofia Kokolaki-Hall

Full House © Lucy Smallbone

Children of the Valley © David Croser

A Cry for Change © PV Mroso

Inca Dreams © Faith Walsh

The Tavern © Sarah Aust

Murder at the Eagle © SW Mackman

Panacea © TB Donne

Tumble Turn © Chris Randall

August Morning © I Robin Irie

Cover design © 2020 Chris Randall

All rights reserved.

Published in Great Britain in 2020 by Moseley Writers Group Press
Birmingham, UK

ISBN: 9798676156022

Dedication

This anthology is dedicated to the past and current chairs of this group both in its current and previous incarnations: Andy Killeen, Katherine D'Souza and Sarah Thomas & Faith Walsh

CONTENTS

	Introduction		i
1	Breakfast in Moseley	Jan Inglis	1
2	Morta	Kathryn Cooper	14
3	Rebirth	Evelyn Kemp	22
4	Document 18	Andrew Brazier	35
5	The Forever Home	Sarah Bartlett	51
6	Perso e Trovato	S.L. Jones	61
7	Osaka Nights	Sofia Kokolaki-Hall	75
8	Full House	Lucy Smallbone	82
9	Children of the Valley	David Croser	90
10	A Cry for Change	P.V. Mroso	108
11	Inca Dreams	Faith Walsh	118
12	The Tavern	Sarah Aust	127
13	Murder at the Eagle	S.W. Mackman	134
14	Panacea	T.B. Donne	143
15	Tumble Turn	Chris Randall	155
16	August Morning	I. Robin Irie	164
	About the Authors		171

Moseley Writers Group

Moseley Writers' Group is a friendly, informal, and supportive writers' group for anybody writing fiction. We meet on the first three Tuesdays of every month, from 8.00 until 10.00, in the cocktail bar at the Prince of Wales pub in Moseley, Birmingham. Come and join us, and sign up for our newsletter by emailing MoseleyWriters@gmail.com

Introduction

'The last thing I wanted was infinite security and to be the place an arrow shoots off from. I wanted change and excitement and to shoot off in all directions myself, like the colored arrows from a Fourth of July rocket.'

Sylvia Plath, *The Bell Jar*

'Nothing is so painful to the human mind as a great and sudden change.'

Mary Shelley, *Frankenstein*

'Turn, Turn, Turn!'

The Byrds, *Turn, Turn, Turn!*

Welcome to this, first ever, anthology of writing by the Moseley Writers Group. As well as being the title, *Changes* is also the theme of this anthology. Change can mean so many different things to different people, and how we deal with change can tell you a lot about yourself. Change can be something we initiate and control. More often it is something unexpected. Embracing the unknown and tackling something new can be very daunting, and the writing within offers a multitude of reasons why change can mean different things in different situations. For some, change is exciting, but for others, it can be extremely unsettling and many aren't capable of adapting to new circumstances.

Moseley, and wider Birmingham beyond, is a place of constant change. New people come and go, new buildings arise while others fall into decay and are forgotten. We may not like it, there's little we can do to stop or delay change happening. - but we do have a choice. In this anthology you will meet characters and situations where this choice is made. In **Breakfast in Moseley** we meet two old friends, ladies who breakfast. There is, however, a darkness between them: the danger of a dangerous an abusive relationship, and the shadow is casts between them. **Morta** is a Roman goddess of death. As Julia and Simon wander through the memorials to lost lives, they reflect on the nature of death, and the changes is can bring - and the consequences.

In **Rebirth** a seemingly genteel world of country houses and well-bred people, something very real breaks through into this world, and compels them to re-evaluate priorities, and for Florence, a new change, and a new opportunity. The discovery of an apparently innocuous **Document 18** leads to an extensive search back through time and forwards into a near future, which has an explosive impact on the legacy of an all too famous President. In **The Forever Home** a man overhears his wife talking dirty to a stranger down the phone. This apparently discovery leads to unexpected revelations and changes to both their lives.

All Emmanuele cares for is his quest for the perfect building for his dream project. Blind to the dangers, he takes on a project which leads to his downfall, and a meeting which tells him the price of choosing gain over love, and the true meaning of **Perso e Trovato.** On holiday in Japan, the narrator of **Osaka Nights:** receives an unexpected gift, and realises she is being watched. In **Full House** two friends break into a strange old, empty house, and find that the house is not as dead as it seems, and hungry. For **The Children of the Valley** change is something they want never to happen - never ever ever. **A Cry for Change** explores how the most trivial change - a birthday - can lead to something much more fundamental. **Inca Dreams** takes you to an ancient civilization, where unwelcome and destructive change looms, but for Huaina, a more blessed and wonderful change awaits. **The Tavern** is where the narrator meet Derek – in unusual circumstances, but which leads to changes in both their lives. In **Murder at the Eagle** writers' group, a murder takes place at a writers' group. Investigations reveal a possible culprit, and a motive concerning jealousy and stolen stories. An important file disappears from Mary's computer, and it proves the catalyst to an exploration of a more fundamental change she is going through. She receives a drug - a **Panacea** - to ease her change, but taking it leads to very unexpected changes. A **Tumble Turn** is what Alex was desperate to do, and to prove to the rest what he can do, but pays the price for the change this brings. On an **August Morning,** on a plantation in 19th century Jamaica, life changes forever for the lives of the families toiling under the merciless sun, and a new life brings new found freedom.

These then, are the sixteen stories, sixteen explorations into the changes we face and the choices we make about them.

David Croser, Elizabeth Tunstall, Chris Randall & Faith Walsh

September 2020

Breakfast in Moseley
Jan Inglis

Every other Saturday my friend and I meet for breakfast at a café in Moseley. It's a great feeling, leaving a kitchen, spotless from its Friday clean, to indulge in luxuries I would never cook for myself. We are ladies who breakfast.

It's quarter of a century since we first met and shared a bachelor girl flat. She's one of those people who can build a social life from scratch, and in doing so she created a bit of a social life for me. She is the only woman I ever met who could pick up, chew up, and discard men without shedding a tear. Of course, she used me. I was the convenient, less attractive, friend to take to social occasions when she was on the look-out for boyfriends. It's not a good feeling, but I tagged along because she was fearless and had a way of making me laugh.

We are both single again. I am widowed and she is divorced. Our freedom to indulge in breakfast out, is because my daughter is at University, and her ex has her kids on alternate weekends. We sit chatting, and to all the world we appear like comfortable old friends. Nobody would guess the unanswered question lurking in the corners of my mind about her part in putting me in danger from a scary boyfriend.

My friend's name is Jane. Her personality requires something more unusual, Zuleika or Zelda. She modified my name from Eve to Eva and then Evita. I think she was being sarcastic. It's hard to imagine someone like me standing on a balcony and setting Argentina on fire.

She breezed back into my life a few months ago when a career move made her return to Birmingham. She found me by contacting my mother. So far, she hasn't tried to drag me along to the middle-aged equivalent of the dreary night clubs she used to like. It was at one of those clubs that I met the scary Robert Deacon, and that didn't end well.

So, I have said Rob's name. For a time, I wouldn't say it. Like my mother wouldn't speak the name of the man who shot John Lennon. My mother still mourns John Lennon. I couldn't care less if Rob is dead or alive. The fact that I had ever fancied myself in love with him horrifies me. At one time, the fact that I told him I loved him, made me want to tear out my own tongue,

At first Rob made me feel beautiful. Perhaps deep down I knew that under all that romantic gush his spontaneity was carefully rehearsed. He told me of his tragic past. How he was never allowed to see his son, the product of a teenage romance. But now I was destined be his strength and comfort.

I cannot even say how he turned me into a nobody. The one thing I can pinpoint, is his habit of finishing my sentences for me, in a bored voice. It made me feel boring. On one occasion Jane witnessed what was happening. She tackled me about it.

'Listen Evie-Evita,' she said. 'I know his type. Things won't get better. Get rid of him.'

I suppose I was angry because I knew she was right, but I didn't get rid of him.

Things came to a head when I got that projectile vomiting bug and asked him to stay away. He was in a very bad mood on our next meeting, when I explained that I had been unable to keep the contraceptive pill down, and we would need to use condoms. He said that condoms spoiled things for him. There was a long silence before he did an extraordinary thing. He took out a photograph and showed it to me.

'I slept with her last night,' he said.

I was not only incapable of speech; I was unable to take in what I was looking at. When I handed it back it could have been a picture of an elephant for all I knew.

'Well, that's it,' I said at last. 'You haven't got what you came for, and you can get it somewhere else, so you may as well go.'

'I'll go when I choose,' he said, and there was something frightening about him. 'You invited me for a meal. A fry up will do.'

Standing over a frying pan was the last thing I felt like, but off I trotted to the kitchen. Thinking now about what happened next is like watching a film. I don't think of the good little girl who carried in that tray as myself.

He was in his misunderstood little boy mode by the time he finished the food.

'I don't know how or why it happens,' he began, in his your-the only-one who-understands voice. 'At the moment there are three girls in love with me.'

I think it was then that my instinct for self-preservation started to kick in.

> 'I don't use condoms,' he continued.
>
> 'We could wait until I'm safe on the pill,' I said.
>
> 'The choice is entirely yours,' he said. 'But if that's what you want, you know where I will go now.'
>
> 'I've already suggested that's what you do,' I said.

He stood up. He took a long time to put on his jacket. As he made for the door, I tried desperately to stop him.

> 'I love you,' I said.

I'm not sure what I was expecting. He turned, and may God rot his guts, counted up to four on his fingers.

I did a lot of crying in the following week, which irritated Jane.

> 'Why do you have to catastrophise everything,' she said. 'You're well rid if you ask me.'
>
> 'That's not the way I feel.'
>
> 'Listen Evita,' she said. 'Toughen up. Think like they do. We all have our needs. You take what you need and as soon as it stops working you get over it.'
>
> 'It was such a horrid ending,' I said
>
> 'It was an odd ending,' she said. 'Why would he be prepared to risk you getting pregnant.'
>
> 'He has a history on that. He was 18 when he got his first girlfriend pregnant. Her parents adopted it. The kid thinks his mother is his big sister, and doesn't even know about Rob. He has no access, and no say in how the boy is brought up. It still upsets him.'
>
> 'My heart bleeds,' she said. 'But right now, you need to think of the future.'

And I did. I started applying all over the place for a better job.

A couple of weeks after the split, Jane dragged me along to a night club with some of her friends. Evidently, I was seen by someone who knew Rob. The next night there was a ring on the doorbell. I was at the door to the landing ready go down to answer the outside door, when the new tenant downstairs answered it first.

> 'Visitor for flat two,' he called upstairs, and Rob came bounding up. He made himself at home, in his usual chair.
>
> 'How's the manhunt going?' he asked.

I didn't know how to answer that, and before I could, Jane appeared with a cup of coffee in her hand.

'Anyone else for coffee?' she asked.

'No thanks,' he said and left.

'Are you sure he dumped you because I'm not,' Jane said. 'Give me a word by word account of the whole thing.'

After I'd gone into every bitter detail she nodded.

'To be honest, it sounds a bit ambiguous to me. He gave you a choice, risk pregnancy or I will go, and you chose for him to go.'

'Do you call that a choice?'

'It was a choice, and what happened was not what he expected. He thought you were under his thumb, and would jump into bed as instructed. Now you've wriggled free. He'd rather think he'd dumped you. If you want shut of him your best bet now, is to appear heartbroken and needy. He'll go, his honour intact. If you still want him, God help you.'

* * *

The next evening when the outside doorbell went it was Jane who went downstairs. I looked out of the window and saw Rob's car. An unexpectedly long length of time passed. I went onto the landing and looked over the banister and saw them together. What I saw was not a I've-lost-my-girlfriend-give-me-a-hug kind of kiss. It was a serious snog. With intent. I staggered back into the flat and sat down. It was Jane who came in first, like someone visiting a sick bed.

'It's Rob,' she said. 'He wants to ask you something.'

I moved from the sofa to the chair Rob usually used. He sat on the sofa and Jane remained standing

'I have a request,' he said.

'Me first,' I said. 'Do you have a photo of me? If you do, I'd like it back.'

His snort of surprise was loaded with contempt. 'No problem,' he said. He stood up and took a wallet from an inside pocket, rifled through it and held something out for me. It was a photograph. As I took it, he held onto it for a fraction of a second. That made me look up at him and our eyes locked. I shrank back in my chair. I had been warned.

He started talking as he stood above me and carried on as he sat down. I couldn't take in what he was asking. I checked that the photo was of me, noticing, with a pang, how happy I looked. The droning of his voice stopped for a moment, as I tore the picture of myself in half. Jane gasped.

Rob talked to me in the tone of a reasonable man humouring an awkward child. He kept reminding me of things I was supposed to already know. That he was close to his friend Mike, that Mike was going to New Zealand, deserved a good send off and had always been friendly to me. None of this was familiar to me, but I didn't argue. He went on to remind me that his flat was small and he had an awkward landlady. I did know that and nodded. Then I realised what he was asking, and couldn't keep the incredulity out of my voice as I spoke to Jane.

'Is he expecting me to throw a party for him in this flat?' I asked.

'We've never had a party here,' said Jane. I knew what this party would mean.

I would spend a couple of days preparing. Rob would bring a new girlfriend, possibly Jane, and on the Sunday, I would clear everything up while Jane slept off her hangover, or worse, spent the morning in bed with Rob. If a committee was formed to devise a way of roughening me up, they could not have suggested anything better.

'It's too much work,' I said.

'I'll do the music,' Jane volunteered.

'We'll all help,' said Rob.

I felt like a mouse between two cats.

'I'm not keen on this idea,' I said. 'But I will think about it. I promise.'

I saw a smirk of triumph on Rob's face.

'But right now, I've work to do for a job interview tomorrow,' I continued. 'So, if you don't mind—'

Jane cleared her throat. Rob sat back as if he had no intention of leaving, and I remembered her advice.

'But it's nice to see you,' I said. 'Perhaps you'd like a drink before you go.'

It worked like magic. He stood up, said he was in a hurry, and left, no doubt satisfied that he'd left me wanting more.

Before he had slammed the downstairs door, Jane had started

laughing. I forced myself to join in. I needed to know what, and for how long. something had been going on between her and Rob, but the questions stayed inside me. I was wary of her now.

'Well done,' Jane said when she stopped laughing. 'He thinks you want him to come round again for an answer. But what was all that business with the photograph?'

'He could use that picture to show another poor girl,' I said. 'I want no part of that. It's only what any woman do isn't it? We girls look after each other, don't we?"
My eyes did not leave her face as I said this. She did not look uncomfortable.

'By the way,' I continued 'You were a long time chatting to him downstairs. Did he say what I'm supposed to have done to make him angry?'

'He said he never knows what you're thinking. You're always so calm and you never argue.'

'He makes sure I daren't argue. Do you think I'm too calm?'

'You were calm tonight considering the brass neck he has asking for a party,' she said. 'But I think we ought to do it. Perhaps he wants to stage a romantic reunion with you at this party.'

'He'll have some unsuspecting girl with him, to slobber all over for my benefit.'

'Then you can be friendly just to show you don't care,' Jane said.
She knew I couldn't do that.

* * *

Next day a miracle happened and I got the job. It would involve more responsibility and more money. My confidence soared and my fear of Rob evaporated as I went home. Going through the city centre I went into a phone box and dialled the number of Rob's workplace. I was about to tell Mr. Robert, everybody's-trying-to-be-my-baby, Deacon what I was thinking.
As he answered, I could hear a background of male voices around him.

'Eve here,' I said. 'You've got a nerve asking me for a

party. Why don't you ask one of your other women? The answer's no, and I don't want to see your ugly mug round my flat again.' I registered some male laughter in the background before I put the phone down.

Jane was out that night. I treated myself to a take away. As I returned to the kitchen with the tray, I heard the downstairs door bang and footsteps come upstairs. It had to be Vic the landlord who lived on the floor above. I hesitated by the door to the landing realising there was loud music coming from Vic's flat. I turned, puzzled, when I heard a key in our lock, because the footsteps hadn't sounded like Jane. The door opened and it was Rob. Perhaps he wasn't expecting me to be behind the door because he looked surprised. Then he started.

'You fucking bitch,' he said.

In panic I threw the tray at him, remnants of the chicken curry and all, and fled. He wasn't expecting that either, because I reached the bathroom and locked myself in before he started to move. He banged on the bathroom door.

'You stupid cow! I've got that stuff all over my trousers!'

'I didn't intend that. I'm sorry.'

'Not as sorry as you're going to be,' he said shaking the door.

I sat on the side of the bath and said nothing. We both waited.

'I need something to wipe myself down,' he said.

'Try the kitchen,' I answered.

He thumped his feet on the floor as he went into the kitchen, but did not quite manage to tiptoe back without a noise. He was there all right, just outside the door.

I climbed into the bath, opened the bathroom window and looked down at the area where the dustbins were. It was a long shot but I called for help.

'For God's sake Eve. What do you think I am?' Rob said using his reasonable adult talking to a child voice. 'I came here to talk.'

I didn't believe that.

'I've never hit a woman in my life.'

I didn't believe that either. It was no use waiting for Jane to come back and help me. There was only one way he could have got keys to this flat and that way was Jane. My best bet was

7

to wait till Vic's music had stopped and start screaming.
Then I heard calling from outside, 'Did someone shout for help?' It was the man from flat one, and he was by the bins.

'I'm locked in the bathroom,' I answered.

Obviously, Rob only heard my voice because he laughed.

'Silly cow,' he shouted. 'You think I'm fooled by that.' He shook the handle again.

'The landlord will come down if you carry on,' I said.

'Not before I've dealt with you.'

By now I was aware of footsteps coming up the stairs, and hoped Rob was in no state to notice. I continued to call out of the window to distract him.

'There's a madman here,' I told the bins. 'He wants to kill me. Get the police.'

'Cut it out Eve. There's no-one there.'

'This is my flat. Piss off and don't come back.'

They were brave words, only made possible by the fact that Vic's music had stopped. But I'd gone too far. As I stood in the bath with only the loo brush to defend myself, Rob started applying his shoulder to the door. Even as I heard movement coming down the stairs, I knew there was a danger Rob would get to me before help arrived. I felt fear in a way I had never felt fear before.

The sound of a key in a lock, and the arrival of help, coincided with another lunge at the door.

'Steady on,' someone called along the corridor, and it was Vic. 'That's criminal damage you're doing to my property.'

'Shit,' said Rob and then, as calm as anything. 'I'm just helping Eve. She's drunk and got herself locked in.'

I got out the bath and opened the door. There stood three men. Vic was a well-built man in his late forties. The man from flat one was in his twenties and had a sporty appearance. He could be called fit in every sense of that word. Rob looked embarrassed and, like an idiot, I felt sorry for him.

'Sorry everyone,' I said. 'I must have had a panic attack and couldn't open the door.'

All three of them looked at the loo brush still in my hand. I gave a nervous giggle.

'You gave us all a fright,' said Rob, tenderly. The little nod of his head told me he appreciated what I'd done to cover for him. That was nice, but not nice enough.

'Thanks everyone,' I said. 'And thanks Rob for bringing back my keys.' I held out my hand for them. 'I won't keep you,' I continued. 'Vic, could you stay a minute I just want a word.'

Rob did not look at me as he reached in his pocket and gave me the keys. The two men stood aside to let him step over the fallen tray and leave. As I apologised to Vic and promised to clear up the mess, I heard the downstairs door slam, and stopped pretending.

'Has he really gone?' I asked.

Mr. Downstairs said he'd check.

'I didn't think you were the type to get into that sort of trouble,' said Vic.

'I'm not. And that's why I'm out of here Vic. I'm giving you notice of three months as agreed, but you won't see me again.

'You ought to give yourself time to think this over,' he said.

It wasn't long after Vic left when the man from flat one knocked on my door. I was cleaning the remains of my supper off the corridor floor.

'Are you all right?' he asked. I opened the door.

'There are less messy ways for a woman to protect herself than a tray of curry,' he said watching me finish off with the mop. I take self-defence classes for women every Friday evening if you're interested.'

'By next Friday I will not be living here,' I told him.

'But thanks anyway, and thanks for coming to my aid.'

'He's chased you away has he?'

'He has.'

'That's a great pity,' he said.

And it was a pity. Mr. downstairs was very nice.

There were two reasons I was surprised when Jane came home early. Firstly, she had her keys with her, and secondly, she had a new boyfriend in tow. They made straight for her bedroom. That gave me privacy to start packing, and I slept better that night knowing that there was a man in the house.

I did a lot of lying over the next few days. I told them at work I was sick, I told Jane I had to visit my mother who was sick, and

I told my parents I'd had a disagreement with Vic. By Friday, I had moved myself and most of my belongings to my parent's house. Jane phoned a few times but then gave up when I said Mum was too ill to be left.

When I told this story to a friend where I work now, she was shocked that I accept Jane, and have never confronted her about what she did. That has made me think. Perhaps this Saturday is the day it will happen. That thought makes me nervous as I get to the café door.

'Evita,' Jane calls out as soon as I'm inside. 'Hurry. I've ordered your eggs benedict to save time.'

'Are you going somewhere later?' I ask.

'No. I've got something to tell you.' She's breathless with excitement. 'Guess who I bumped into at New Street Station last Saturday?'

And I know what she is going to say. And I know today will be the day.

'Not Rob Deacon,' I say.

'My God! You're telepathic! How do you know that?'

'Just a hunch. What was he doing in New Street Station?'

'He was taking his grandson to a match. His grandson! How can that be? Rob's only a couple of years older than us.'

'My daughter's 20. I could easily be a grandmother.'

'But this is a proper lad,' she protests. 'He's going to secondary school next year. Rob is very proud of him.'

'When we knew Rob, his long-lost son was about 8. That would put him in his early 30's now. If he's anything like Rob, he doesn't use condoms, and he could easily have a ten-year-old son.'

We both laugh and my feelings are mixed. If this grandson is who I think he is, it means that at some point Rob did link up with his son, and has enough of a bond with him to be trusted with the grandson. It would be hypocrisy to say I'm happy for him, but I do feel the world is a safer place if Rob Deacon is content.

'I can't get over that you guessed it was Rob' says Jane.

'Who else would we both remember from the old

days?'

'He's memorable all right,' she says. 'Do you know, that cheeky bugger slapped me once.'

'Serve you right for fucking him when he was still my boyfriend,' I say, and her jaw drops.

'Sorry Evita. You weren't supposed to know about that.'

'Why did you pretend not to like him?'

'I didn't like him. I couldn't understand what you saw in him. I just thought he might be a really great shag and worth a try.'

And now I'm caught by one of those fits of laughter that can't be stopped. And she makes it worse by joining in.

'Seriously though, I was wasting my time. He only wanted to get to you. He hit me when I couldn't tell him where you were.'

'I'm sorry,' I say. And I mean it

'I nearly got my own back,' she says.

Suddenly her elbow is on the table, hand pointing upwards, and she's pointing to the base of her little finger.

'See that joint,' she says. 'It's the weakest in the body and if you yank that to the side it dislocates and it's agony. I learnt that from Jamie, the man in flat one. Went along to his classes to try my luck.'

'Did you get lucky?'

She smiles, and now I'm jealous.

One night we went to the pub and Rob was there. While Jamie was at the bar Rob sat in his chair and started chatting me up. Sorry babe and all that. I offered him my hand to shake, and took his hand in both mine.'

I'm cringing now. 'Oh no. Don't tell me,' I say. 'You didn't,

'I did. Yanked his finger to the side as hard as I could.'

'You live too dangerously. What happened?'

'Nothing. He did look a bit startled though.'

It's hard to get my words out for laughter but I have to say it. 'Perhaps he thought it was some sort of erotic message.'

'It's not what he thought that matters. Jamie was on his way back to the table and knew exactly what I was doing.

He banned me from the classes. Said he did what he did to help women in immediate danger, not to have idiots go round settling old scores. Anyway, Rob made himself scarce. I got the impression those two didn't like each other. Not sure why.'

'I can tell you that,' I say. 'Remember the night you gave Rob the keys to our flat so he could come round and beat me up?'

Her jaw drops again and she looks puzzled.

'Come on,' I say. 'When I said there would be no party, you gave him duplicate keys and he came round and let himself in.'

Her face changes and she looks sheepish. 'I did get some keys made for him. I arranged my flexitime so that I could get away on days you were working late and we could--you know. Sometimes he arrived before me and didn't like waiting. Sorry.'

'How long did it carry on?'

'Not long. You messed it up for us when you got that vomiting thing and were off work. After that it was a dreary off and on affair. Come to think of it, I don't remember getting those keys back. Sneaky bugger always rang the bell when he came to see you so that you didn't realise.'

'He didn't that night.'

'Are you actually saying he got in and beat you up?'

For the second time in a week I tell the story. But somehow the story has changed. She's a very different audience to my workmate.

'You threw a tray of curry at him! Brilliant. I hope it was Vindaloo.'

'It wasn't, and there was hardly any left.,' I tell her before continuing. It's hard for me to get upset when I get to the part where I'm locked in the bathroom. She's grinning too much.

'One thing I'll say for Vic. When he fits a bolt, it stays fixed,' she says.

It's not long before she interrupts again.

'A loo brush! What were you going to do with that for God's sake?'

'Please let me finish?'

And I tell her the rest. It's the same story as last time I told it, but this time it's more farce than tragedy.

'What a picture!' she says when I've finished. You in the bath, standing like Boudica in her carriage, brandishing your trusty loo brush, while Jamie leaps upstairs to Vic to get the keys. Brilliant.'
There's a pause in the conversation as I see her thinking.

'I'm glad we had this talk. There was a barrier between us before. Listen, I've had an invitation to a brilliant party in London and I can take a friend. You'll love it.'
I know here's no chance of that. Marriage to Douglas, even though it was cut short, has made me a stronger person.

'No,' I say. 'Why not take a man.'

'Coals to Newcastle,' she says.

'Would you like to come to my bridge club sometimes?' I ask.

Her face changes. Then, 'Perhaps we ought to stick to these breakfasts together,' she says. And that's fine by me.
I like the way my story has transformed from high drama to farce, but some things don't change

Morta
Kathryn Cooper

She stood in the entrance hall, as if waiting for them. Sun pouring in from the overhead window illuminated her outline, giving lustre and life to the smooth, speckled marble. Flowing robes cascaded over slender curves. Curls thick as rope were held back from an aquiline face.

As the queue shuffled forward, Julia could see her more closely. The scissors in her right hand, a spindle in her left. The strand of thread that snaked up from the spindle, crossed behind her body and fell to the floor, passing between the long blades of the scissors.

Simon fidgeted beside her, glaring at the couple arguing with the woman in the ticket booth. The discussion with the attendant behind the glass was in rapid Italian, punctuated by frequent gesticulations.

'Oh, for God's sake, how long does it take to buy a bloody ticket!' Simon's irritation radiated towards her in waves.

'Simon?'

He turned to her; his face still contorted by a frown.

'What is that?' She pointed over at the marble frieze.

He glanced quickly at the wall in front of them. 'A bas-relief.'

'I know it's a bas-relief, but who is it?' She asked.

His eyes narrowed in quick concentration. 'Morta, goddess of death. One of the parcae, spinners of fate. When she snipped your thread with her scissors – that was it.' He turned away from her quickly, back to the queue.

Morta. Julia stared at the calm, dispassionate face, the hand poised casually mid-air, the thread powerless between the blades. Just one flick of those fingers, and snip.

The arguing couple suddenly had their tickets, the man holding them aloft as if in victory. The queue inched forward again, but as Julia followed, a gust of fatigue left her legs trembling, her knees buckling, in its wake.

'I need to sit down.' She said, pointing to the bench on the wall opposite.

Simon nodded, still distracted. 'Ok.'

The muscles in her legs melted onto the seat in relief, as the cool of the marble permeated through. The friezes lining the entrance hall were crowded, dizzying displays of soldiers in battle scenes, swords held high, horses with gnashing teeth, and the vanquished, with expressions of terror and pain, trampled underneath. Julia closed her eyes, tried to shut them out. Tried to will her muscles back into congruity, calm the racing of her heart. Sounds became muffled, a low murmur of voices, the door opening and closing bringing with it a waft of warm air. Traffic on the main road muted, a low roar, like waves on a distant beach. She let herself drift, follow unconscious memories. This time last year. The swirl, and weight, of her graduation robes as she clutched her doctorate, squinting in the sunshine, her face still pinched from too many days reading, rereading, typing and editing. But happy, so happy, as Simon swung her up and around, his face close to hers, close enough to kiss her.

'Congratulations darling!' He had cried, but his arms had been too tight as he held her, his feet clumsy, and careless, as he trod on her hat, blown off by the wind.

The light shifted. Julia opened her eyes. Simon was standing over her clutching their tickets.

'She thought I was your father.' He looked back at the woman in the booth.

She could see it had stung. The assumption happened more often here, where their differences seemed more stark, harder to camouflage, than in the flow and familiarity of life back home.

He came back to himself.

'Are you ok?'

She nodded.

'Yes. I just needed a minute.'

He moved from foot to foot restlessly, glancing from Julia, to the door into the museum.

'Are you sure you're up for this?' His tone aimed for sympathy, but he kept his gaze on the entrance.

'Yes.'

She stood up, defying the weakness in her legs.

'Let's go.'

He nodded, relieved.

'You'll enjoy it.'

He looked uncertain.

'Or, you could just sit in the sun, or, perhaps the shade. There's an amazing courtyard.'

He smiled, his tone familiar, cajoling.

'You will love the garden.'

She tried to smile.

'It's ok. You've sold it to me. Just don't go too fast.'

They entered a long hall of statues, their footsteps echoing on the mosaic floor. Sunlight flooded through the glass ceiling, bathing the marble figures below, casting a lifelike sheen over the stone. Lined up on either side, they stood formally, as if waiting to greet them. Julia walked slowly, plinth to plinth, compelled somehow, to study each one; the poised young men with chest, arm and thigh muscles tightly defined, the still, passive, women in flowing robes, and the busts of older men, staring gravely into some unknown past. Many were incomplete, the rough edges where limbs, heads or features were missing, giving them a strange, wounded air.

'Who are they?' Julia asked, resisting the urge to touch the smooth limbs, the carefully hewn faces.

'Deities, mostly.' Simon answered, 'the Romans loved their gods.' He sounded bored.

'And the others?'

'Famous people; emperors like Augustus - that's him over there,' he pointed to a bust on the opposite side.

He let go of her arm, and moved on, impatient. She was holding him back.

'And these?'

She had reached the middle of the room. The statues here were less idealised, more like ordinary people; people like themselves.

'Funerary statues for putting on monuments or sarcophagi'.

Simon's voice echoed from far down the corridor, as he headed towards the sunshine.

'So, they were real people?' She called after him, looking at their still faces, blank, unseeing eyes. Is that why they are so compelling she wondered? Because we can feel the connection?

She found Simon outside, leaning against a pillar which faced into a large courtyard.

He was talking on his phone.

'No. Don't do that. Yes, I'll talk to him.'

He paused, frowning.

'I said I would.'

An expanse of green stretched out in front of her, the tall white columns on either side, flanking her like sentries.

'Aren't you listening? I said I would, and I will!'

Simon's voice echoed around the cloister as he walked away, his shoulders tense, the phone at his ear. He shook his head as he spoke, his movements punctuated by sharp, incoherent, fragments of conversation.

She sat down on the low wall between the columns. The vast lawn was divided into segments by small diagonal hedges. Trees and shrubs clustered into each section, with statues, just visible through the foliage, scattered throughout. Cypress, and privet, Scotch pine, olive and palm. She felt a rush of pleasure in recognising them, as if they were old friends.

Simon returned, his face set in a frown.

'What's going on?'

She turned her face back to the garden, to a tree with a rotund trunk, and tiny, prickly leaves, that she couldn't quite identify. He stood in front of her, blocking out the sun.

'Tom. He's talking about quitting uni again.'

'Was that Elizabeth?'

She kept her tone neutral.

'Yes.'

Elizabeth. Julia felt the weight of the name, like a stone thrown between them. She edged her way around Simon and looked for her anonymous tree. It was somewhere near the stream of water, being thrown up into the air by an invisible fountain. Elizabeth had phoned every day since they'd arrived, this new saga proving to be particularly fertile. Tom, Simon's younger son, who had struggled to pass his 'A' levels, was now finding uni impossible. Julia didn't know what to say. Over the last few days, the arguments had worn themselves out by repetition. Besides, he wasn't her son. She felt a strong stab of loss. Her son.

Simon paced like an animal between the columns.

'I said I'd speak to him. What more can I do? Perhaps I should speak to Matt.'

Julia found it hard to think of Simon's sons, Tom and Matt. Tall, broad and loud; they blasted through life like supernovas, devouring everything in their path.

'I think I'll go down into the garden.'

She hungered for the simplicity of greenery in front of her; the grass and plants, trees and shrubs. Their internal directives were uncomplicated; without guile, or malice, violence or memory. They just were. She got to her feet, but staggered, the building opposite moving from side to side, the walls blurring around the edges.

'Jules. Please sit down. Rest up for a bit.'

He made it sound like an order she had not yet complied with. He softened his tone.

'We can spend all afternoon here.'

He was still holding his phone, as if expecting it to ring.

'No.'

She wanted to wander among those trees, touch the knots in the bark, look up through the leaves into the sunlight. Feel the sharp texture of the late summer grass beneath her feet.

But a closer look at the rows of uneven marble blocks lining the paths and lawns, revealed them to be gravestones and sarcophagi. Her heart sank. More death. Even on the inscriptions on the stones nearest to her, tall Latin letters and dates, crammed onto the stone with no spaces in between. The names of the deceased.

'Ok,' she said sitting back down. 'But let's not stay too long.'

Simon looked at his watch, distracted.

'When will you phone him, Tom?' she asked.

'Not now. When we're back at the hotel.'

He slipped his phone into the pocket of his shorts, but kept tapping it, as if for reassurance.

He wouldn't meet her eye.

'Can you give me an hour? I'm meeting one of the curators upstairs to check out some new epigraphy. You stay here in the shade.'

This too was familiar. There was always someone to meet up with, something new to see, and discuss. Julia closed her eyes against the brightness of the sun, thought back to their conversation last week.

'Rome in September' he had said, 'it might be just what you need.'

Had he really said that? Her memory of the last few months was vague and shifted, like sand blowing on a beach. What was clear and obvious at one moment, was easily obscured the next. Had he actually wanted her to come with him to this conference, or had she imagined it?

It had been a mistake. Sightseeing on her own, in the last few days, she had been dazed by the snarling traffic which circled their hotel, and most of the city, and found the ancient sites startling in their intensity. Everywhere she looked were images of war, sword upon shield, the agony of the fallen and the exultant, edgy faces of the victors. Violence bubbled under the surface of every pathway of the city like a hidden stream. Even her pilgrimage to the Villa Borghese gardens had brought no relief, the grass dried, and sharp under her feet, the trees limp and exhausted from the heat.

She watched him walk quickly along the cloister to the staircase inside. From this distance, his skinny frame and loping walk made him seem youthful still, despite his greying hair. Once she had been drawn to that energy, happy to sit in his slipstream, to be part of his world. Now she wondered if she had been naïve, a side-act in his circus; vying for her turn in the spotlight while others waited in the wings.

She stood up finally, hot and drained, as the sun hit this side of the cloisters, her legs numb from sitting so long. It was almost midday. Simon had been gone for over an hour. She headed back towards the main museum, but stopped when she saw a family coming towards her. The father, a man in his thirties, transported a baby in a complicated carry frame, the tiny child perched aloft, like an eaglet in an eyrie. His partner, carrying a rucksack almost as big as herself, pushed a buggy alongside him, another child scampering in front. She turned into a doorway unable to bear their tight, tense smiles, the undercurrent of smugness, her sudden desolation.

It was a small shadowy room lit by flickering half-lights on the walls. Deprived of sunlight, it was dank and musty; the coolness, clammy. A large rectangular sepulchre stood in the centre. Instinctively, Julia ran her fingers over the swells, curves and dips of the intricately carved marble, tracing the patterns of cherubs and vines, fruit and flowers, thinking of the people who had carved this, so precisely, so long ago. And the people who had commissioned it. She started, hadn't noticed the baby, smooth and perfect, lying curled on the flat roof, almost hidden by shadow. The inscription 'T.F. Theageno, antequam nascantur morientium', the translation leaping out at her: Stillborn. She sat down heavily on the plinth, closed her eyes, as to ward off the grief that still oscillated down the centuries.

A 'late miscarriage', it was called; a confusing term, that created a vacuum, that no one knew how to fill. Stillbirth, only weeks apart, they would understand.

Simon had not wanted to, but she had held him, Michael, swaddled in a cotton wrap, his eyes fused shut, his skin shiny and taut, dusky from the veins just under the surface. He had been so light, light enough to float away. What would it have taken to ground him, to keep him here?

She closed her eyes, fell into darkness. Floated down on a smooth, mellow tide, her muscles unfolding, fatigue dissolving. Resigned herself to weightlessness, suspension, being held in a timeless void, like life just before birth, just before death.

Sounds intruded, disjointed, and jarring. A rapid heartbeat. A baby, crying. A woman calling her name. Simon. They became more insistent, then faded. A shadow passed in front of her; a glint of scissors, a swish of long robes, before drifting away.

She came to on the floor, her brain still clouded by grey mist, her dreams still lurking. A face appeared; solid and square, assured, an attendant, her dark hair pulled back tightly, her lipstick crimson, a strong musky perfume.

'You will be all right. Just rest.'

Her English was heavily accented.

'Jules.'

Simon emerged from the shadows, a strained look on his face.

'Are you ok?' he said.

A pillow felt soft under her head, the woollen blanket heavy on her legs.

'What happened?'

'You fainted. Perhaps from the heat,' the attendant said,

looking towards Simon. 'Perhaps from your anaemia.'

Julia looked up at the dim lights on the wall, the sarcophagus in the corner, shivered a little.

'I want to go home.'

She looked for Simon's expression in the gloom.

'Ok.'

She could sense his hesitation.

'If you want.'

'Are you coming with me?' she asked.

He hesitated.

'Well, there are still a few things I need to do here.'

He was already glancing around, anxious to move on.

She had finally recognised the feeling of abandonment. He has left me, she thought, behind a wall of grief, as heavy and impenetrable as that stone tomb.

'Ok.'

A cog in the machine slipped finally into place. Everything moved on to a new position where there was no turning back.

'I'll see you back at the flat though eh, in a few days?'

He smiled his old smile.

She took his hand, felt the familiar grooves and ridges of his fingers and palm. There were many forms of death she thought. Accepting change was the only chance to live.

'No. I don't think so, Simon.'

Rebirth
Evelyn Kemp

'Florence!' a voice called.

'Huh?' I jolted in surprise and plastered a fake, broad smile on my face as my heart pounded with such ferocity that I had to take a deep gasp of air to compensate.

'You should know how much I hate a lady using words like that! It's so inelegant and unfeminine. Your papa and I brought you up far better than that, and of course that wonderful finishing school you attended. It's just so common and you, my dear are certainly not that!' My Mother chastised me tapping her fan off my hand in time with each word.

I would've rolled my eyes if I hadn't been sitting in the garden veranda with my Mother and her fellow socialite friends. They were the very top of high society and most were members of Mothers' bridge group as well, and the other half would sell their daughters to belong to that elite yet small group.

I stood slowly and smiled at the group of women, forcing myself to be as polite and happy as I could. 'Please excuse me ladies, I need to use the powder room.' I turned and slowly walked past the maids, trying to stop my legs shaking uncontrollably and back into the house when my Mama's voice stopped me in my tracks.

'Florence hasn't been the same since she came back home. I believe we should continue with our little arrangement,' my mother spoke while her friends giggled.

My mother could sanction murder and her ladies would swallow every spoonful they were fed.

'You're right of course, my dear.'

I recognised the voice as belonging to my grandmother, the Duchess, Lady Cecily.

Without being scrutinised under their prying looks anymore, I finally took the opportunity to sigh and roll my eyes.

'What are those vultures planning next? 'I muttered as I walked into the house to retrieve my book and curl up on the window seat in the parlour.

'I'm home!' my father called.

I glanced up at the clock and leapt up to greet him. I couldn't believe how long I'd spent reading!

'Hello, Papa!' I beamed at him. 'Can I get you anything?'

He leaned towards me and lightly planted a kiss on my cheek.

'Hello, Florence, dear, you look lovely today, is that dress new?'

His eyes sparkled with mischief as he winked at me.

'Really, Papa, now you're just being silly. It's old but I embroidered some flowers on it. We don't have enough rationing coupons for new clothes.'

'You did a most fantastic job! Where's your Mama?' he asked, linking his arm through mine.

'Mama and her ladies are in the garden; I came in to read my book.'

'Oh, your Mama and her flock of birds.'

'Grandmama is here too.'

'Really? The Duchess herself, to what do we owe the honour?'

'I don't know, Papa.'

My Father's butler, a chap called Edgar hovered nearby ready to assist.

'Ah hello, Edgar. Could you get my slippers and pipe for me? Oh, and a pot of a tea and the newspaper. I'll take them in my office.'

'Of course, sir.'

Edgar turned and walked off.

'I'll see you at dinner later on then, Florrie?'

Papa lifted my hand and lightly kissed it.

'Yes, I'll see you at dinner.'

I smiled.

'Oh, my dear daughter, I meant to ask, what are you reading?'

'Mansfield Park by Jane Austen, Papa.' I lied, while smiling broadly at him.

'I'm so very glad your Auntie Alice gave those collections of books to you.'

I said nothing but smiled; he leaned towards me, touched my

elbow lightly and started to walk away.

'Oh Florrie, Your Mama said to dress appropriately for dinner tonight; apparently we're receiving guests.'

He winked at me again, his eyes lit up jokingly. My Father and I had always been very close but recently we'd started to drift apart. I think he still thought of me as his little Princess but in my head, I felt like I had crawled my way through hell and back.

I lowered my head in polite acceptance as I turned into the parlour and retrieved my book from where I'd hidden it. I held the solid paper mass in my fingers, and rotated it slowly, my hands were still red raw from all the carbolic soap I'd come into contact with, in situations outside the family, my Mama insisted I wear elbow high gloves to cover my 'unsightly' hands. I stared at the cover of the book; it was a nursing pamphlet that had been mass produced by the Red Cross for the Civil Nursing Reserve.

'Miss Florence?'

I stuffed the book at the back of the bookcase and stood up.

'Yes! I'm in the parlour,' I called back.

'Mistress said it was time to draw you a bath and help you get ready for dinner tonight.'

My maid, Nellie, appeared in the parlour.

'Alright then, thank you Nellie.'

As we climbed the stairs together, Nellie, who was walking a respectable few steps behind me, started chattering.

'It's so good to have you home again, Miss Florence, the staff, including myself were all so worried about you, Mrs Browne was lighting candles in every window for you, until the air raid warden gave her a right ticking off. She was so embarrassed!'

I felt so deflated, a few years ago I would've been impressed with that story and teased Mrs Browne at every possible opportunity but now, I simply felt nothing.

'Thank you, Nellie.' I attempted a smile. 'I can do the rest by myself.'

I closed the door shut before she had chance to protest, I wanted to be by myself, I could fend for myself, I'd demonstrated that, if nothing else, over the past six years.

Wrapped up in the warm, scratchy and starchy towels after my bath, I headed for my bedroom and closed the door behind me. My wardrobe doors were open; I smiled; Nellie must have laid out something for me to wear. I dried my skin slowly and applied the moisturiser that Mother had got for me to try and fix my hands.

I slowly padded over to the open wardrobe door; and smiled to myself having that bath had almost altered my outlook completely. Maybe I could wear that teal suit that had been Mamas', or that dress that Grandmama gifted me.

My brain was whirring away thinking of potential outfit ideas, shoes, handbags and accessories when my eyes finally focused on what was in the wardrobe in front of me.

I heard a soul shattering scream and stepped away from the closet while my heart hammered with such force it threatened to leap out of my throat. It was then that I realised the scream was emitting from me.

'Florence!'

My father shouted as he ran over to grab me forcefully by the arms. I lifted my arm and pointed at the offending item in my wardrobe. My brown nurses uniform complete with barely visible blood stains, you could barely see them but I remembered exactly where they were, the same as I vividly remembered the men whose blood had left those stains.

I sank to the floor with my hands in my eyes as the memories started again.

John, Jack, Eric, Tom, Bill.

I breathed out slowly and shakily as I attempted to recompose myself.

John, Jack, Eric, Tom, Bill.

'Get rid of that!' My father screamed at the maids who had gathered at my bedroom door, no doubt summoned by my scream.

'Come on, Florence, get up. Our guests are downstairs already and no doubt, they've heard your little display.'

Sniffling I stood up slowly and shakily, my eyes downcast as my face burned with shame.

'Yes, Papa.'

'Nellie, come and help Miss Florence get dressed and we'll see you in the parlour room in fifteen minutes.'

'Yes, Mr Edward-Jennings,' said Nellie, bobbing a tiny

courtesy.
Nellie stuffed me into my prettiest Elizabeth Arden dress and manhandled my hair into a presentable style.

My father returned to collect and escort me to the dining room, as we stood waiting for Edgar to announce that we were here my father lifted his hand to push a strand of hair off my forehead.

'No more silliness tonight, Flo, yes?'

I smiled and nodded, putting a fake smile on my face. They couldn't understand what I had been through.

'Good girl.'

He patted my cheek lightly.

'Your sister is here as well with her husband.'

'Really?' I whispered, and my heart lifted slightly.

'Florrie!'

I span around sharply.

'Cecile!' I exclaimed excitedly.

We ran towards each other and embraced. It was the first time I'd seen my sister since I'd been back home. I felt a single tear escape my eyes and slide down my face.

'Look at you!' I cried as I pressed my hands against her swelling stomach. 'I can't believe I'm going to be an auntie!'

'Have you lost weight? When was the last time you had your hair cut? Ooh, I like your gloves!'

I opened my mouth to respond but Cecile's husband walked toward us.

'Florrie, this is my husband, Edward Spencer.'

'It's a pleasure to make your acquaintance, Mr Spencer.' I smiled demurely.

'Oh please, call me Teddy, we're family now.'

The fake smile remained on my face. We'd been family for several years but this was the first time we'd actually met. I'd known about my sister being married through her letters when she wrote to me during the war. It had caused a slight scandal in the community when they were first wed, because it was so unusual for the younger sister to marry before the elder, but I was in Belgium at the time.

'I have the pleasure of announcing The Right Honourable Henry Edward-Jennings and his daughters Florence and Cecile, Mrs Edward Spencer and her husband!' Edgar's voice boomed as the dining room drawers swung open. I hated this act, this foolish attempt at social hierarchies, primping, preening and make up. It made me sick. I had seen the very worst of humanity, and it had rendered all of this so very trivial.

'May I introduce Mr Albert Delaval, eldest son of Mr Cuthbert Delaval, the property magnate, and Mr William Percy, eldest son of Aloysius Percy the tenth Duke of Northumberland,'

My sister and I curtseyed prettily and were promptly shown to our seats; I was situated between our two male guests. As soon as my back touched the cool leather of the chair it dawned on me, they were trying to arrange my marriage. I cringed inwardly.

'What was that screaming we heard? Are you quite alright, my dear?' my mother asked.

'Florence saw a rat.'

My father spoke on my behalf.

The guests around the table laughed in unison.

'Was it a large rat?' William Percy asked as the laughter continued.

'Huge.' I responded sardonically. 'Biggest rat I've ever seen in my life.'

I wanted to stand up and to shout at them, to tell them the horrors I'd come face to face with but instead I settled for gritting my teeth in annoyance.

'Cheer up, Florrie; you look like you're chewing a bumblebee!'

My sister laughed.

'Your Mama was saying you were a nurse during the war?' Albert asked me, quickly changing the subject.

'Yes!'

I swallowed some wine quickly.

'I was stationed at the 76th general hospital in Liege in Belgium.'

'Oh I say. You brave thing! Wasn't that the one that was bombed? I heard about that in dispatches, I must say, I spent most of the war in France myself.'

I nodded and opened my mouth to speak.

'Albert,' my mother chided, 'this is not the time or the place for such gruesome and grisly talk. Please, not in front of the ladies!'

'But of course, I'm forgetting my manners. You may call me Bertie, Mrs Edward-Jennings.'

The rest of the dinner continued in a similar tone, we chatted idly about the weather, sports, gardening and my mother's ridiculous plan to present me to society, even though in my opinion I was far too old.

'Mama, debs are presented up until the age of twenty-one, I'm twenty-six, I'm far too old!' I argued.

'Twenty-six and not married yet, you'll end up a spinster at this rate!' William Percy joked.

I bit down on my tongue to stop myself say talking and attempted to smile instead.

'I just haven't had the fortune to meet the right man...yet,' I responded politely.

'No I imagine most of the chaps you met during the war were dead!'

He cracked yet another joke as I debated cracking my plate over his overly coiffed hair.

'So, Miss Edward-Jennings...' Bertie started, interrupting William.

'You can call me Florence, if you wish.'

Bertie breathed a sigh of relief and a smile slowly spread across his face, he leaned closer to me and spoke quietly.

'What made you want to go into nursing, Miss... Florence?'

He corrected himself quickly.

'I wanted to help people, I saw how much death and destruction was going on and I figured it was the right thing to do. To try and help as much as I could.'

'Florence, Bertie no whispering at the table, it's dreadfully bad manners!'

My mother admonished us like we were children.

'I apologise Mrs Edward-Jennings, I only asked after the dressmaker of Miss Edward-Jennings dress, I was looking

for gift ideas for my cousin's wife,' he lied convincingly, broadly smiling and showing his perfect straight white teeth.
A smile started to slowly creep across my face, perhaps happiness did exist in my future.

At the end of the meal, I calculated where William Percy's foot was before I pushed my chair back to stand so the chair leg deliberately came down right on his left foot.

'Ouch! Bloody hell!' he exclaimed loudly as Cecile, Mama and I gasped at his profanity.
I placed my gloved hand in front of my mouth and tried my hardest not to giggle.

'Language, Mr Percy!' Papa warned.

'Oh Mr Percy, I am so sorry, how very careless of me! I am so, so sorry. Are you quite well?'

'I'll live,' he responded coldly.

'I'll have one of the servants get you a cold compress and we'll sit in my office and discuss the state of the world. Shall we?' Papa asked our guests.
Before the gentlemen retired to Papa's office to drink brandy, smoke cigars and talk about god only knows what, Bertie approached me.

'I have something for you,' he said, his voice so low that I had to strain my ears to hear him.

'You have something for me?' I repeated like a confused parrot.
He nodded slightly, proceeded to take something out of the inside pocket of his jacket and handed it to me.

'Do not read it now, read it later when you're alone,' he instructed.
I took the paper, folded it again and slid it into the top of my gloves.

'It's been a pleasure to meet you, Florence, thank you for the service that you performed for our country. It would be my greatest wish to meet you again and call on you sometime.' Bertie returned his voice to its normal volume.

'I would like that too, Bertie,' I said sincerely.
He kissed my gloved hand and turned leaving the dining room.

'I should like to retire for night now,' I told the remainder of the ladies.
Cecile came and threw her arms around me, holding me in a

tight embrace, well the best she was able to with her pregnant belly getting in the way.

'Teddy and I are staying here for the night so we'll be able to talk more in the morning. I want to know all of your adventures! Did you have any romantic dalliances with soldiers? Did you go to dances and have lots of friends? Your letters were so sparse!'

'Goodnight, Cecile.'

I kissed her forehead lightly as I too left the dining room.

I hurried to get to my room; eager to see what Bertie had given me. The minute the door was closed I snatched the paper out from its hiding place. It was a leaflet advertising a group meeting for those who were struggling to readjust to life since the ending of the war, and those men who were dealing with shellshock. It was definitely worth a secret trip. As I climbed into bed my brain went into overdrive almost immediately, recalling the names and faces of all those men who had lost their lives while I cared for them.

John, Jack, Eric, Tom, Bill.

I took a deep breath but it did nothing to hinder my terror and anxiety.

John, Jack, Eric, Tom, Bill.

'Stop it! Stop it! Please stop it!' I hissed through sobs as I pulled the quilt over my head in an attempt to abate the thoughts.

I must have dozed off eventually because the next thing I remember was Nellie flying in to my room with such force I was surprised the door didn't come tearing off the hinges as it collided with the stone wall.

'Miss Florence! Miss Florence! You must get up!'

She hurled my dressing gown towards me.

I sat upright slowly. Was I dreaming, and was this real?

'Mrs Spencer has gone into labour and the midwife is unable to visit!' Nellie screamed in hysteria.

'Nellie, get me some towels and some hot water, can you do that?'

Nellie nodded slowly.

'What do I need you to get?' I reminded her.

'Towels and hot water... towels and hot water,' she stuttered.

'Well done, Nell.'

I shoved my arms forcefully into the dressing gown and ran towards my sister's rooms as fast as I could.

Cecile's door was already open, her husband, Teddy, was pacing in slow tormented anguish.

'Right, Teddy, you go with Papa to the drawing room, play cards, smoke some cigars or do something else to keep you both entertained. Mama, you're with me.'

I turned to my sister's attendant, a young pretty girl by the name of Maeve.

'Maeve, take a taxi and get to the midwife and bring her here as soon as she's able. Failing that, we can always take Cecile to the hospital in Papa's car.'

I donned my authoritative nurse's voice; it felt like I'd never forgotten how to use it.

'Fine.'

Papa took Teddy's arm and led him away as Maeve also left the room.

As soon as Nellie had returned with the towels I had, yet another, job for her.

'Nellie, get some alcohol, vodka, possibly. Go! Now!'

She turned and speedily left.

'Cecile, sweetheart, Cecile, listen to me, please.'

My sister turned her eyes on me, she look petrified and writhed with pain and terror.

'The child isn't due for six weeks, it's far too early, it won't survive. Will it be okay?'

'Do not fret, my dear, worrying is bad for the child. I need to check the baby is in the right position, it may be uncomfortable but Mama will hold your hands and mop your brow.'

I turned to our mother and gestured towards the bed with my eyes. Mama's hands flew to her throat like a worried bird but, after I threatened her with my eyes, she did as I asked and perched on the bed and took Cecile's hand. I breathed a sigh of relief and uttered a quiet prayer to God that, thankfully, the child was in the correct position in the birthing canal.

'Cecile, we need to time how far your contractions are apart, the closer they are the quicker the babe will be here.'

I soon realised that the contractions were coming very close together; this baby was coming far quicker than I had hoped. I'd only been present at two births but I'd never delivered one by hand, not that I planned to admit that to my family! Cecile let out a soul shattering scream that ricocheted through my very being, it made me want to vomit. I swallowed down my nausea; I could do this for my sister, I would do it.

'Cecile, on your next contraction I want you to push as hard as you can, I want you to scream as you push. Can you do that for me?'
My little sister nodded as sweat slowly meandered down her brow.

'Your next contraction should be coming in about thirty seconds. When it starts, I want you to push, alright?'
I glanced at my wristwatch as I repeated myself, making sure my words made it through the pain and mania.

'It's coming, Florence! Help!'
'Push, my love, push!'
Cecile screamed again and I saw the crown of my niece or nephews head.

'I can see the head!' I cried, 'You're doing amazingly, first time babies can come very quickly and I think this little one won't leave us waiting for long. It'll be over soon, Cecile, I promise.'
The promise escaped my lips before the reminder leapt into my head, a matron had told us once never to make promises to our patients, but I wouldn't go back on my word now.
I heard a crash behind me as I span round to see a woman, who I could only assume to be the midwife, standing in the doorway. She threw off her outer clothes and rushed over towards me and elbowed me sharply out of the way.

'Thank you for keeping the situation under control for me but I'll take it from here.'

'No!' Cecile whispered. 'Can't my sister stay with me?'

'You may choose, Mrs Spencer; your Mother or your sister.'

'I'll leave, Cecile. I'll be down the corridor if you need

me.'

I touched my sisters' face and started to leave the bedroom.

'She's all yours,' I muttered quietly as I walked away, the woman's tone upset me deeply but I refused to let the old battleaxe see it.

I returned to my room, and for once, sleep came easily and my nightmares stayed away.

The first thing to wake me the following morning was a shrill cry, shoving me forcefully out of my peaceful slumber.

'What the...?' I muttered as the memories of last night came rushing back like a tidal wave.

Cecile. The baby. I flung the quilt back and dragged my dressing gown on from where I'd haphazardly abandoned it the night before and ran down the hallway, not caring about my hands or my appearance.

I burst into my sister's room with the force of small female tornado.

'Florence, I'd like you to meet your niece, her name is Flora-Mae Catherine Spencer. Flora-Mae, this is your auntie, Florence. We named her for you and Mama.'

My sister spoke quietly cradling a little bundle.

My mouth opened and closed several times but I couldn't find any words to explain fully how I felt. My hand moved up to my cheek to wipe away tears.

'May I hold her?' I eventually managed to croak out.

Cecile nodded as I perched on the edge of the bed and she passed the child over to me.

'Cecile, she is so, so beautiful. You did so well. I'm so very proud of you.'

I leaned over and pressed my lips against my niece's forehead and then my sisters.

'She's like you, of course she's beautiful,' Cecile responded.

'I'll come back and see you both soon. Can I get you anything from town? Tell you what; I'll get you something to surprise you.'

I sniffed; my emotions had gotten the better of me.

I ran in my bare feet back to my room, quickly pushed

myself into some clothes, attempted to make myself look respectable and pulled my gloves on. I had my mission now. I slipped my hat on as I walked out of the front door and down the steps to the pavement. I let out a breath that I didn't know I'd been holding on to and smiled. I glanced at my wristwatch, I had fifteen minutes to reach my destination. At a slow yet steady pace I ambled my way to the city centre of London, as I walked, I watched the cities buildings being rebuilt as people tried to readjust to life after the war.

The church of St. Michael's of all Angels loomed in front of me, I tugged at the old church door and stepped inside and headed to a small room at the nave of the church.
The door was already opening, a group of people, mostly men, were sat on chairs talking amongst themselves. They all turned towards me as I walked in.
I saw Bertie, his smile broadening when he saw me, in response I gave a bashful, socially self-conscious wave and then silently cursed myself for being so awkward.
'Hello! You must be Florence?'
An impeccably dressed man walked towards me, I assumed him to be the organizer of the group.
'Yes, I'm Florence Edward-Jennings,' I replied as we shook hands.
'I'm David. Welcome to the group.'

Document 18
Andrew Brazier

She flicked the turf of mostly dark hair, a thatch of cross matched threads, away from her eyes. She didn't want to slip. Her bare feet skipped down the wooden steps two at a time. Despite her thirty - cough cough - years, she felt like a child in search of Santa's booty. Admittedly what she was looking for wouldn't be wrapped in pretty paper – but the sense of freedom was immense. Two weeks ago, she would have had to wait, shower and dress; precautions against the inevitable intrusions by the greatest horror - other people. Now the public library was closed. Now the world had changed again. Now she could peruse the paper paradise in paddy feet and a T-shirt nightie that was almost a museum piece itself.

She danced down the aisles of history that teetered and bulged from the forties metal frame shelving. With a few twinges reminding her that not everything was still childlike – she replanted herself on the floor by the heap she deserted last night. Encouraged that the gloves, sealed tubs and face mask, would still be there in the morning, she had accepted defeat. This was the treasure trove, the mother-load – here she felt were the answers needed for her book. Here she had begun to prove her view of this borough, Windmill Hill. The lockdown had other advantages too. All too often she would be digging in some ancient box, when a tube train would vibrate the dust of the decades onto her hair, clothes – and mysteriously often into her packed lunch. This time, the tube had stopped too.

This enforced peace allowed for another aspect of her research. She liked to talk to the files: egging them on to relinquish their hidden facts and chiding them when they made her sneeze. Her files, her archive, her library. Be afraid all ye who would enter here – her flag was planted, the kingdom of Kathy. Rules of entry: 'keep your mitts off the pretty papers!' A gift, and at least a lockdown's notice in advance, was the minimum requirement for free passage. It was all she could do to stop herself ripping the word public off the archive sign. The prize, oh yes it was here somewhere, would be proving the existence of 'Win.'

'I know you're in here somewhere, you old bag,' she exhorted.

The problem was that any document before the age of printing were one-offs, fragile to the point of disintegration, and likely to only still be in the archive because they weren't that exciting. She had to find electricity by rubbing primitive sticks together.

For five hundred years the area had been quarried and, just as the world got bored of flint, they found enough iron to spawn a village industry in shoeing horses. Then finally, as the world changed again and fired all the horses, Windmill Hill found coal for the industrial revolution. Such a history was common and Kathy's books on various similar topics had sold well enough to buy the flat over the archive. This particular version of English history, though, had a ghost. A figure who appeared in so much local folk lore that you could barely enter a pub without being told to, 'beware the ghost of Win.' As a historian she never pointed out to them that as Win had probably lived, if at all, in the fourteen-hundreds, their nice Georgian hostelry was unlikely to be host to her ghost – unless Win was posthumously an inebriate of staggering propensity. What was more likely was that she had built a windmill at the top of the quarry that had given the area its name.

No, the point was that such a character would probably have been based on someone real. If proven, the provee would be sitting on a human-interest story, a search for bones under car parks akin to the seeking of Richard of York, and hopefully a TV series starring someone other than her. The tales would have it that she was a self-interested, determined old boot, who had seen off wars, men, and apparently death. An icon for feminism and potentially an early exponent of free love, Win had caused a lot of trouble. To which end, Kathy loved her. In fact, Win was Kathy's ideal person, heightened by her deadness. All she needed to do was prove she existed. Her chances of proving it were increasing with every day the lockdown lasted. Admittedly, she was getting precariously close to going feral, but this was important research. Inspired by progress, and the image of her wild self, she ran back up to the flat to find a music source, and breakfast.

By lunch time she was head-banging between 'Financial records, non-ledger 1401 – 1499' and the provocatively named, *unlisted documents*. Having lived all but her university years in the area and frequenting the library during college days – she had been in this corner a few times before. Admittedly not always for academic purposes. Twenty years ago, this was a good place to drag a partner. Each futile fun encounter an attempt to balance out her desire to get physical with the abhorrent idea of being in a relationship. Even back then the dates would last roughly for as long as it took them to start wanting to have conversations. She had stuff to do, and if they wanted to fit round it, then they could stay. Otherwise they could sod off with their expectations and social niceties. More recently, still happily single and lured by a friend in to trying online dating, she had dented one of the sets of shelves during an energetic celebration of buying the flat. The man had been dispensed with quickly, but the dent would still be here somewhere.

In the fourteen-hundreds it was mostly church records, which had joyous calligraphy, and often a flourish in the language. Not, the marriage ended badly in scandal but, *tôgêare orgilde ûser heofonweard hiere of hê gêmung nêan unêaðelicnes*. Sometimes, if you were lucky, a record of a financial deal might remain. What she needed was a birth or death record, that would be enough. She knew what she was doing, she knew what she was looking for, and she could see the dent from the exploits with Malcolm. Whilst so far Win of the Windmill remained elusive, the pictures painted by the albeit sparse documents were lighting up like a pageant.

Around dinner time, a loose concept based on a brief retrieval of sandwiches and a beer, Kathy saw it. At approximately eight of the clock, this day of lockdown number fourteen, she found it. A landowner named something like Hamilton noted a sale, which seemed to tally with the land mentioned in the unnamed document of last night. Whilst the buyer remained a mystery –

it referenced a large country house some forty miles away. The country house still existed and was National Trust owned. A few phone calls to a locked down enthusiast might produce something concrete. A new possibility had come to light which would connect the dots beyond the tired velum. What if Win was known at the manor? Not as a paper trace, but as a character in their story. Tomorrow she would make calls and send emails. Tomorrow she would cook real food and work from the flat - well, for a little while at least. Tidying up, she lovingly placed the papers back in the sealable tub, neatly added annotations to the lid with sticky labels, and started pushing the box back onto the shelf. A creaky settling indicated that the shelves were pleased to have their load returned.

'I'll be back, don't you worry. You'll be famous yet.'

She had barely turned away when the shelves made a skittering sound, then a solid snap noise as something hit the ground. Her experience told her that a file had slipped out and sneaked down the back of a rack. Still, it had startled her a little, but as she headed for the likely source, she knew exactly what to expect. Probably a later document, post war, not kept in a sealed box but a manilla file, shaken loose by her activity, would be wedged between racks C and D on the second aisle. Reaching down and behind she could feel it. Carefully wiggling her fingers, she edged it along until it could be grabbed. A duller piece of flotsam you could not imagine. Government offices had a million of these. They usually contained a plethora of off-white paper, the names and addresses of a few seemingly random people and details of an event that no longer mattered. This one had the slight saving grace of a few colour photos and a document with a government stamp on it. So, it was relatively modern, but looking older because of council regulation paper and a reused folder from the fifties. With something of the air of a professional golfer playing nine holes on a pitch and putt, she prepared to tackle the mystery. Finding a table, retrieving the kettle from upstairs, and settling down with a cake in a box that had been delivered earlier, she celebrated her success by figuring out where this miscreant belonged.

If serious archive hunting in your nightie is the ultimate in hedonism, then a misfiled document is the ultimate sin. As if she was investigating a crime she put back on a pair of the non-latex gloves, then spread the contents in an arc. She opened the plastic wallets that contained the photographs. This was hardly the stuff of her work. This was just for fun. Putting the photographs aside, she tried to ascertain the general department of the library that these should be stored in. Not only were these too recent for her work, they were far too recent to be in this room at all. If the fifteenth century took up a couple of boxes then the Victorian era, took up vast acres. The Victorians, it seemed, were as bad with records as the modern generation was with social media: a ton of pointless trivia, presented as if it were fascinating and poignant.

'Maudy and I attended church in the landau before the picnic,' was no more news than, 'The cake I made! Woohoo.'

The efforts of those self-egotists drowned any real history and pushed the post war era down a corridor and two flights of stairs.

'You cheeky little thing,' she berated. 'Upgrading yourself so shamelessly. You are playing a long way from home.'

She meticulously noted the phrase, 'gold-digging rack climber' on a post it. Sometimes these phrases were useful to spice up her publications.

She started having a half memory of a file like this; of modern papers disguised in old packaging. The image that had jumped into her head was the sticky sweet fear of being caught by the stern librarian. Something about this file made her feel like that. Maybe it was the caffeine and sugar rush, but was she once caught with a file she wasn't allowed? Hardly likely as people generally gave her free reign and encouraged her to be here. They called her 'The hermit,' but no one would think to stop her doing whatever she liked – well academically at least. In addition, this was not an exciting file. Fun yes to be poking her nose in, but hardly a thing of fear. This was silly. Turning to the photographs she flicked through, making sure to check the notes on the back. There were more than fifty of them, but the third drew her attention because the woman in it had some similarity to her. Standing with a dog and a very smiley average looking guy, was someone who could have been her. Younger, yes, but a remarkably close likeness. A photo of a relative perhaps? On the reverse she found an additional shock; a simple note stating Catherine Bailey, Cardigan Bay 2021.

'You can't spell it dear,' she said out loud.

She was Bewley, and definitely Kathy with a K, but the tension was back.

The whole thing didn't make sense; similar name and appearance and dated only six years ago? The photo looked much older than that. Did she have a sister perhaps? A sister who was married with a dog - well that was a reunion she could miss. She was just going for the mobile phone to call mum, when she spotted another picture of the 'nice young man' but this time alone. Behind this boyfriend was a banner stating, 'Lockdown conspiracy - tell us the truth.'

She, and the rest of the world no doubt, would never forget the revelations, protests and endless politicking of the virus conspiracy. She had protested herself and cheered when the government fell. She recalled the endless headlines about the second lockdown being faked - for its environmental benefits. The banner in the picture looked about right. The anger was at the deception and not the reason. 'Trust the people,' hers had said. It suddenly amused her that these days it was treated as a kind of international sabbatical.

'Where are you locking down this year?' she mimicked a friend with a posh voice.

'I'm staying here, book to finish you know,' she replied as a satirically dull version of herself.

It was true though, lockdowns had become quite the fashion,

and the environment did get a break. The simplest analysis was usually the most accurate. Clearly the photos were dated wrongly.

'You nearly had me fooled! I should be better than this,' she said kindly to the snap-shot. Absent-mindedly she looked at the government stamped missive. Document eighteen, as it was titled, was a set of minutes for a meeting.

'Well you are thrilling aren't you. Do I really care that David Clarke gave his apologies? I am thinking probably no. Who are you, little bastard escapee?'

Abruptly she realized that the date on the document confirmed the dates on the photos. It was marked 'amended/changed 1st June 2021.' She began to feel quite anxious. Was this really a set of pictures of people protesting about the 'fake,' lockdown before it even happened? As a historian this could be quite a find, but also left her hand on a smoking gun. Did she want to be that person, the informer?

She knew she had to be more methodical about this. She was reacting before the facts were proven.

'Calm down idiot. Mr file, please would you give me something more solid. You are slightly freaking me out here.'

This Malcolm, the name on the back of photo four, would have been considered a prophet. The similarity in name to her casual encounter niggled too. She wondered if she was dreaming - overcome by sleepless nights and the endless hours in boxes. Greater researchers than her had been found high on fumes in crypts, tripping on spore dust or the lack of clean air.

Picture by picture she began delving. The papers, including the minutes in document eighteen, were largely unhelpful. Just updates on the installation of new office equipment and the re-election of council staff. Not even the names meant anything to her. By image ten though, the photos began to talk – and they weren't saying anything nice. On the back of one was a last seen date. On another the word 'deceased.' Plenty of them just showed groups of protestors in front of police cordons, and a name or two on the back. Later in the pile, as the penny dropped, Kathy became fairly sure of what she was looking at - and that these prophets or perpetrators had been 'disappeared' to stop them talking. In 2021 some people tried to stop the government and they were silenced. This was a scandal of huge implication.

The last few pictures left her paralyzed and fighting for breath. She tried desperately not to panic. Instead of the original protest they showed a handful of the individuals caught candidly going about their lives. These ones had the words 'found' or 'seen' on the back and a date. Three of them, just three of them were dated in the future. On the last, a single defiant black man faced the camera holding a card. It read 'I know it's 2031 - FUCK your TRUTH.' On the back, with the minimalism of government efficiency it stated, 'S. Samuel Geneva WHO protest. Arrested. She watched the occasional car potter past, no doubt returning to some lockdown paradise they'd arranged, wishing reality would kick back in. She felt cold, exposed, and frightened. Worst of all, she was beginning to think she already knew something about this. A lifetime studying history told her - clearly - that a found document was unlikely to be misdated three times unless it was a deliberate act. One way or another she was facing the very real possibility that finding Win wasn't the discovery she was about to be known for.

'What the hell are you doing here young lady?'

Utterly lost she spun to see the security guard looking puzzled. It was all she could do not leave a puddle on the parquet flooring.

'My archive! Mine! Shit, George, you bloody arse. I am allowed to be here. I nearly pissed myself! What are you doing here?'

'Kathy? What the fuck happened to you? I had a report of a wild woman trashing the library.'

She was grubby, ashamed and humiliated. She couldn't

remember when she'd last washed, or even seen herself in the mirror.

'I got a bit wrapped up in the research.'

'Well, I am not one to judge – but you have looked better.'

Without asking he walked over and put the kettle on.

'Is there anything I can do?'

'No, yes, fuck – maybe. I'm panicking!'

'I can tell!'

George had been the security guard for a long time. Kathy knew his story, teacher at the college, beautiful Nigerian wife who died, so left with time on his hands. 'Actually, could you hang around for a bit. I might need your perspective on something. I'm going to shower and get some clothes on. This is going to sound weird, but can I trust you.' She was almost begging.

'You've known me long enough.'

Shortly after, safely clad in jeans and jumper, she sat with the oddly welcome presence of this other human. She explained what had happened. He listened and thumbed through the photos as she caught him up.

'So, after the virus,' he checked.

'Yes, but before the fake shut down.'

'Well, if they had been disappeared, Boris would have been having kittens. He did lose his job around then I think?'

He traded for a new set of photos. Kathy kept her mouth shut as he approached the one that looked like her.

'What is this?' he challenged.

'One of the photos - what do you think?' She tried not to let her frightened eyes give the game away. Independent verification was needed.

'It's you!'

'Well she looks a little like me, I thought a relative maybe.'

George took a pair of reading glasses from a top pocket and peered closely at it. 'No, love, it is you. Even if I wasn't sure, look at the T-shirt.'

'Shit, it's my ...'

'Yep, the one you were almost wearing.'

'But I have no recollection ...'

'Yeah - I mean yeah,' confirmed George.

For a while they sat and drank tea while the enormity of the discovery began to sink in. Maybe age, or the death of his wife, had trained George to approach problems calmly. For a brief while he was everything she wasn't. They began to pull all the possibilities apart, looking for the most likely explanation. Day faded, pizza was ordered, and diagrams were drawn. In the early hours of the morning, the old man and the hermit agreed that they might have a theory.

'So, assuming the file is real, do you believe that this is evidence of something strange?' she asked.

George looked at her as steadily as he could muster.

'I am not sure what I am seeing, but I believe you have found something. I also think that to fake something like this would be difficult - and sinister in its own right.'

Kathy summarised. 'I'm going to read this to you, and you are going to stop me if anything I say doesn't fit with what we have seen. If you don't say anything, then from tomorrow we try and prove it.' George nodded. After reading it through twice, they reluctantly agreed that, despite its enormity, there wasn't really any other explanation. That perhaps history had been amended, that there had been many more lockdowns than anyone could recall. That people like herself had spotted the problem but had been silenced. That the lockdowns were covering something far more twisted than either the original virus or any environmental concerns. It seemed likely that, changing their names and lives, these rebels had planted information to remind themselves of the truth. That many many people had had years stolen from their lives and memories. That finally and most personally, that they themselves were probably considerably older than they thought. Shaking with the shock, Kathy concluded, 'So we start looking, we can scan the internet for information...'

'No, no, wait. If this is what we think it is, we mustn't be discovered. Anything we search for on the net has to be disguised as research for your book or something. There will be trackers everywhere, searching for these topics. No, we are going to have to print out manual files, we're ...'

Suddenly a thought hit him.

'You already put this into your own head. You didn't just hide the file; you hid the means to find it and research it. You search alone, in manual files, for a person called 'Win.' You're a famous historian, and you are swanning about in the sewer that is Windmill Hill. Don't you see, you planted the seed to find yourself. That is why you've been so driven to find her. Seriously, you are searching for Windy Miller? Is your next project, 'is Trumpton real?' You've left yourself some clues to chase.'

Over the weeks that followed they set up a system. Each day George would cover his tracks around the town and eventually pick up food to bring to the library. During the first week they did nothing but establish the problems that would exist if you screwed with time: memory, births, deaths and marriages, manipulating figures across vast numbers, and knowing how any fake information would be taken. During the second week they solved how to cover their tracks on the internet. Changing laptops, only beginning each check from the 1400s, and constantly running false searches for stuff they didn't need.

By the fourth week of what Kathy was still referring to as the sixth lockdown, despite all the evidence, the floor was completely covered. Diagrams, records, statistics and photographs hung from every surface. Sitting in the very epicentre of the storm, she felt like each nerve in her body was connected to a lightening-storm. Her mind was working at its absolute best and she had the instrument of success in her hand; a ten-meter steel tape measure. All she needed was George to sound off to, and he was late. She stared at the door trying to evoke his presence. As he walked in, she jumped up and exclaimed, 'I found it.'

George looked like he was about to drop the pizza. 'Evidence?'

'What we were looking for – I have the proof.'

'I know we had ideas, but seriously – proof?'

'I found 'Win!''

Extending the tape measure, she made him catch the other end. 'I know it's difficult with the crap on the floor, but edge across until you make it a straight line from where the picture of Malcolm is on that shelf and where I am in the middle. Ok, cool, that is close enough. Now take it down to the floor. I laid everything we found in time order. That wall is Jan 2020. That wall is now. So, this should be the general stats for everything during that period.'

George obviously couldn't see it yet.

'It all looks similar. There is no obvious blip.'

'Exactly. Look closely, from where the ruler is. Get closer – on your knees.'

'Leave off! I'm old!'

'Please, just get close. I won't make you do this anymore ok. This is it. If you can see it too, then I am not mad. But I can't show you. You've got to see it. Pick a line, any line. Births, marriages, population, local, national. Then very slowly look up the line to me. These ones near me are the manual files from this library. These are the ones you dragged up the stairs.'

For a little while the room became so still that a beetle marching into to 2024 made them jump. Then, as she watched him intently, his body language changed. From searching to a stiff alertness; subtle but readable.

'These are too neat. They are managed numbers. The paper records have slight mistakes. There,' he pointed to a bundled-up set of newspapers and tracking data for the election in 2020. I remember the news. They stopped counting because – because ...'

Kathy jumped in, 'there was a power cut. The opposition woman, um, anyway she conceded. They finished the count days later. Someone obviously forgot to add them onto that graph.'

'Yes, and in 2021, there are at least three different figures for ....'

George was back on his feet.

'Before 2021 those look like those,' he said pointing to the papers from the vault. 'Can I cross this?'

'Yes, I photographed it all. This was just so you could see. I've started on charting measures for each group of anomalies with matching lack of errors after this point.'

She was still pointing at the line when he reached her island. Then she was hugging him.

'I'm really scared.'

'We are in a load of shit,' said George. 'So, what was

the actual proof. This is flimsy by your standards.'

Without letting go she explained.

'It was you who said it actually. You said we had to be careful about being tracked. Once I had a specific date for the changes, I looked at our laptops. Often the cookies use W I N, as in windows file. I think I had already been told this in the past and chose the character to remind me. Look,' she broke the embrace and pulled the old man across to the table, 'you showed me when we looked at the computer history stuff. File eighteen, document eighteen, introduction of Windows Eleven was mentioned in the minutes of that stupid meeting. Amended 1st June 2021. Guess what the amendment was? The offices of the Borough Council would need to be ready for the change to Windows Eleven. The tracking cookies were hidden in there. From then on, whoever did this, could change the dates, times and events to fit ... well to make it look like whatever they wanted it to.

'Surely people not using Windows?'

George was battling the magnitude of what he was seeing.

'Social media, people passing on files, it wouldn't have taken long. Anyway, none of it would change people's memories – for that we are back with that symptom from the virus in the Congo. Look I don't have everything, but I have enough. Some expert in computers will identify the tracker in Windows Eleven, and I can tally that with the line in the statistics.'

She slumped into the nearest chair. For a long time, they sat and watched out of the window as pretty much nothing happened. In a few days they'd put all this out into the world. Litter every media possibility, write letters, and warn the world. There is only one response to finding you have been screwed out of years of life.

'Pizza?' George offered.

'Yep. What've we got.'

'I got a Pepperoni and Texas BBQ. I fancied a change.'

Entry 116521: International Court of Justice. Document Eighteen. The court acknowledged the actions of Katherine Bewley in uncovering the missing information. Her work on the 'Win Virus' and the crimes against humanity committed during the so called 'missing years' has been seminal in bringing the prosecution.

The court accepted the defences mitigation that the intention of the various individuals was laudable, and that the motivation for the instigation of a drastic environmental strategy was not for personal gain. This said, the use of eugenics, mass menticide, deception, use of a bioweapon, proven acts of false imprisonment, and causing the loss of liberty, constituted crimes against humanity. The court rejected the charge of genocide on the grounds that, whilst the sum of human loss was on a scale commensurate with genocide, no deaths could be directly attributed to the crimes listed.

In summing up Judge Jeffreys stated, 'We have long held dear to a modern myth that the super-villain was the purview of the cinema. This incident wakes us up to the reality that a group of ultra-wealthy, highly motivated, and deeply disturbed individuals could instigate a crime on this scale. Unlike Hollywood, we failed to save the day. Even more alarmingly, the crime remained undetected for fifteen years. The key aspects of the charges; the complete and blatant disregard of human rights, democracy and personal liberty, undermine the nature of life. Such an act requires new laws, and a new awareness of how much power we give any one individual.'

Appendix 11a: 'Trumpton-trojan.' Although former president Trump was implicated, no proof was ever received directly relating him to the 'missing years crime.'

A lesser charge of 'international fraud' was brought and proven. President Trump died three months into a fifteen-year sentence; still denying that the 'fake news' experiments and programmes were linked to the events of 2020/2021.

The Forever Home
Sarah Bartlett

The day after I overheard my wife talking dirty down the phone to someone, I presumed to be her lover – I'd quickly ruled out a side hustle in the sex industry given her out-and-out snobbery – I fully expected to find her in the kitchen when I got home. With an explanation, hopefully. With a bit of an atmosphere, almost definitely. But that evening, for the first time in our married lives, she wasn't there.

I'd fallen into a nightly ritual of grabbing a beer when I got in from work, slumping into my armchair in front of The One Show, letting the celebrity interviews drown out the interrogations of the working day. I'd hear Lois clattering about in the kitchen while our teenage sons did whatever they did up in their rooms.

And now, as I opened the fridge and looked blankly at the beer, I wondered what I might not have heard in the kitchen night after night. Lois flitting and flirting around Facebook maybe, furtively checking her online running-away fund, or swiping at some random man, while the vegetables boiled.

Lois had never worked, well not since that job on the cosmetics counter at Boots in the early days. She had only ever known security and comfort, stepping from her parents' five-bedroomed house to our starter home in a nearby estate, newly married to a policeman with prospects. She soon she swapped her retail career path for the more lucrative returns of the property ladder, and we barely had time to enjoy one house before moving up another rung.

I'd left home early that previous night, and as soon as I walked into the kitchen she put her phone down on the worktop. She didn't say a word, and to give her credit, she generally made the effort when it came to conversation, teasing out the details of my working life. She'd have been great at interrogation. But this time nothing. 'You do not have to say anything. But it may harm your defence if you do not mention....' I walked past her, eyeline straight ahead, took a beer from the fridge and disappeared into the living room, my mind in mid-crash.

This morning at work, Jim caught me doodling in a case meeting. Startled, I looked down at my notes and was horrified to see how untidy the page was. I paid attention from that point, but when the meeting ended, I took an early lunch so I could sit on my own in the canteen and work out what to do. I stared down at my pasty and beans and wished I'd waited for my mates.

Back at home, it was time to take action, so I abandoned my feet-up, beer and TV session for my own missing person investigation, to open up our domestic trappings room by room. God knows where Lois was, but at least she wouldn't get in the way.

The kids were in their rooms – I could hear the whirrs and bangs of their computer games – and there was no reason to disturb them. I started in the spare room, checking that all the suitcases were there. And yes, her passport was in the bureau on the landing, with the others. I gave Lois credit for being smart enough to keep our master bedroom clear of her shenanigans, whatever they were.

I was running out of ideas, and looked down at my phone to see if she'd called. Then I remembered that she sometimes slept in the guest room when her teeth-grinding kept me awake.

The guest room was immaculate of course, like every area of the house. Even the boys' rooms got a fortnightly deep clean. I sat on the duvet and looked around at all the cushions and candles. Lois spent hours and hours every month consulting the latest House & Garden magazine. The boys renewed her subscription every Christmas, which saved them the job of putting some real thought into their gifts. She had a pile of back copies by the downstairs toilet and the current issue in the lounge.

It felt like I was no longer enough for her. Why did she need excitement all of a sudden? The Lois I knew never craved excitement. The boys couldn't drag her on to the lamest of rollercoasters. She was like me, grounded. We worked well together. We planned what we wanted and decided how to get it. We made a good team, even my mum said that. I'd given her everything her friends had. Wasn't that the key to happiness, to have everything in common with the people around you?

We met on the same night that her best friend Mandy met her future husband, my best mate Mick, in a pub in Solihull. Our engagement party two years later was crammed into the calendar with all the other engagement parties. Lois and Mandy were each other's bridesmaids, and even went through their first pregnancies together. We did family holidays together in Corfu.

I checked my phone again. Should I try calling her? Should I bollocks. It wasn't me who was in the wrong.

It was Lois who drove that agenda of getting what everyone else had. I followed suit though - stretching the mortgage to buy our forever home; shopping for a new bathroom suite while the paint was still drying in the kitchen; endless rounds of home improvements. But she was on her own when she chose steam-cleaning the carpets over Sunday morning sex when both boys were away on sleepovers one weekend.

Yes, when was that weekend? It might have been around that time that she met her lover. A wave of nausea passed over me. Come on, Steve, I said to myself, you're good at this. My working memory made me a star on every investigation I'd ever been part of. But just when I needed them most, the neural connections turned into dead ends. I started to understand why happily married detectives outperformed the singletons, even when we had babies screaming for attention every hour of the night.

The phone rang and I jumped. Was it her? I picked it up. It was Mick.

> 'Mate! We're going down to the Bull's Head tonight.

We've all got passes.'

They all needed permission from their wives for a night out. Just like I usually did.

'Coming out? It's an eight o'clock start.'

There was no indication that Mick knew anything was wrong. Even though our wives ran an information network that would put GCHQ to shame, mainly on that WhatsApp group of theirs.

'I'm in,' I said.

I needed to get out of this fucking house and stop waiting for Lois to come back.

It's funny how we can feel someone's absence. That nano-drop in temperature when one human being is missing and the silence you can almost hear. A silence that should have been filled with the clink of crockery and the drivetime radio DJ in the kitchen.

But instead of the comforting sounds of family life, what drifted into the silence was Lois's voice, in breathy tones I hadn't heard for years. '...until you come all over me'. I felt a bit nauseous. Had she been watching porn on her phone? Throughout our marriage, I'd only ever come in one place.

I looked at my phone, again, to check whether she'd called, again. That's when it hit me, and I knew where to find the clues I needed. Wherever Lois went, she took her phone with her, so no chance there, but her iPad would be in the house. I walked back into our bedroom, and there it was, in her bedside drawer. I entered a PIN, and as I guessed, it was the same as her debit card. So any old clown could get into our online bank account and drain us dry. All that police budget that went on detecting high-tech fraud would be better spent on good old-fashioned public information films, I'd often thought that.

I swiped my way through three or four screens of app icons. No WhatsApp, but there was Facebook. Playing home detective had come natural to me so far, but now came the ethical struggle. I'd always respected my wife's privacy, And the kids'. We'd never been the type of parents who went prying into their children's rooms, rooting through drawers, leafing through diaries. I had to force my trembling finger down on the Messenger app.

And there he was. Right at the top of the list. 'No, I just can't do it, Jack,' I read. 17:46 the previous day, just after I caught her at it. I scrolled down further, but the thread told me nothing about what she couldn't do, or what she already had done for that matter. Whatever it was had been discussed verbally or even face to face. But I did know that his name was Jack, and he was a barista in Solihull. Christ alive. I'd like to see him pay off her monthly soft furnishing bills. I flung the iPad on the bed and stood up.

The boys were going downstairs as they always did at this time, triggered by the expectation of food, like a pair of Pavlov's dogs. I put the iPad back where I found it and followed them down. Time for that beer. Maybe she'd said something to them about her whereabouts, but I couldn't bring myself to raise the alarm by asking. I was desperate to keep up the normality for as long as possible, just in case she walked into the house with a palatable explanation I could at least pretend to believe.

Unlike Mick and my other mates, I did know how to cook. Not just the blokeish stuff like carving and barbecues. I could do burgers, fry-ups, all sorts of things. Surveying the fridge, I found three pizzas. Why not four? That would do though. Who needed Lois? Well, to tell me where the pizza cutter was for a start. And to find the paracetamols because Sam had one of his gaming headaches from all that gunfire (a career in the Royal Marines did not await, whatever he thought).

Half past seven and there was still no sign of Lois, and I wasn't about to mention her. Then Jamie asked if she'd gone out for early doors. I nearly spat out my beer. 'Women don't do early doors,' I said. 'What's sauce for the goose is sauce for the gander, Dad,' he retorted. Where the hell had he got that from?

'Anyway, I think she said she was dropping something off at your Gran's,' I said, ignoring his politically correct swipe. Fuck knows what I'd do if Gran rang.

'I'm off soon,' I continued. 'Do you think you can hold the fort while I'm out?' They nodded, neither of them looking up from their pizzas. Tomorrow morning they'd open fire with a barrage of questions if Lois was still not back. Christ, I'd tell them the truth now if I knew what the truth was. Instead, I was only one page ahead of them, if that, like a supply teacher in a sink school. I prayed for the sound of a key in the front door lock or her car on the gravel. And then I booked an Uber.

At eight o'clock exactly I was jostling my way through the Friday night crowd at the Bull's Head. People were standing in clusters, most of them younger than me and oblivious to anyone around them.

I remembered meeting Lois on a night like this. She was chatting with a group of girls. I still know them all. Those big dark eyes of hers. Long brown hair in big, bouncy curls. She was pretty and popular. She fitted the bill. I stared.

Her friends noticed, of course. We were all of an age when group radar is permanently switched on, in the search for life partners. The girl next to her was Annie, one of our battalion of bridesmaids two years later, and next to her was Mandy, who nudged Annie in the ribs and started giggling. The entire group turned to me, and as my face burned up, I hurried to the bar, where I peered into the back-wall mirror to see what she was drinking. It looked like a white wine spritzer.

Like fuck was I going to chat her up in front of all her friends. Leaving my pint on the bar I walked back, and looking her in the eyes for just one second I said, 'This is for you', and handed her the spritzer. Half an hour later, Lois and her friends materialised right next to me and my mates. Mandy struck up a conversation with Mick, and ten months later Lois and I were engaged.

By now, I'd made it across the pub to my mates, stationed at the end of the bar as they were every Friday night, hobnobbing with the landlord as off-duty policemen do. Time to leave the navel-gazing behind – normality is what us blokes do best. Mick was mid-joke when I arrived, and there was a pint of bitter waiting for me on the bar. I gave the landlord, Brian, a quick nod and got stuck into my beer.

This was my territory. It was unchanging, unchallenged. I was one of them, I always had been. Everything about me blended in, right down to my beer belly. We would all be loath to admit it – old-school police officers like us don't do psychobabble – but this pub was our safe space. Although I'd left street patrolling behind years ago, investigation work brought you into just as much conflict. You needed a haven, a chance to decompress. My cosy domestic setup had gone AWOL, and I was clinging to my mates like they were the only lifeboat in a storm.

Laughter. The joke was over. I tuned in.

'How's Crowther?' I asked, to establish my own presence more than anything. Tim Crowther was the lead officer on an investigation a couple of them were working on, and there was usually a story to tell about his latest fuck-up.

'I don't know about Crowther, but have you heard the latest? Four officers set up some kind of porn studio on a canal boat they commandeered.'

'A crime scene?' I asked.

'No, not that bad, but get this. They got some unemployed cameraman to film those sex scenes, every weekend apparently. And they only stored the footage on the station server!'

Amateur porn. Telephone sex. I couldn't get away from sleaze. Where in God's name had Lois got to? I glanced at my phone. Did she and her friends have some kind of safe house they could disappear to whenever they felt like it? Nothing would surprise me. One or two of them had 'married well', as they say, one to a surgeon at the Priory in Edgbaston. Were they all syphoning money into a runaway flat? Probably not, I decided. The reality was likely to be a more sordid affair - a three-star hotel on an arterial road.

I'd drifted off. They'd soon notice if I did too much of that. The whole evening was about avoiding suspicion. This lot were ten times more vigilant than Sam and Jamie. My professional inner voice screamed out that forced normality was often the most suspect behaviour of all, but it was all I had.

Who was most likely to have twigged? My eyes swept the group. Nick and Tommo didn't even notice me looking at them, which ruled them out. Brian the landlord was performing his usual routine - laughing at jokes, keeping the regulars happy, with his eyes constantly surveilling the large crowded pub for disturbances. He wasn't one of those landlords who left it all to the bouncers. He'd have been great on duty at a football match, especially if Millwall were playing away.

Mick though. He met my eyes and then looked down at his pint. He knew, alright. That time Lois got caught shoplifting at John Lewis, well, it was never going to be Primark, he found out before I did, thanks to his gossiping wife who was there when it happened. But for now, Mick didn't seem to have breathed a word.

Lois clammed up whenever I probed her about the shoplifting. My boss kept it out of the courts and the local newspapers. She might have rewarded me with an explanation, but it was never forthcoming. Her GP prescribed anti-depressants. I did wonder at the time whether it was all the hours I was working, and of course the problem had only got worse. The austerity cuts meant the working day was even longer, as we tried to fill the gaps our former colleagues had left behind.

Maybe I'd join the ranks of the divorced saddos who stalked their offices for available sex. I felt hollow just thinking about it, and the only remedy I could think of was to get a round in. I turned away from my mates and moved to the bar to get served. In any other pub I would have to work hard to get the barmaid's attention. But not here. Not on my patch.

I felt a dull shove in my left side and jumped to attention. I'd drifted off again instead of focusing. Some little bastard was leaning right into me, trying to force himself to the front of the bar. Surely Brian was on the case though. This little runt wouldn't get the better of me, not with the people I mixed with.

I felt the strangest compulsion as he pushed himself forward, blocking my access to the barmaid. A physical sensation, an energy that was growing inside me, from my gut right down my limbs and through to my fingers. I couldn't contain it, this force that was pushing me towards him and without even thinking, I grabbed his straggly hair and pushed his little pin head right down on to the bar. It felt natural. Easy.

That was better. Whatever that destructive energy was that had built up inside me had gone away. Dissolved.

I noticed blood streaming out of his nostrils and into the bar towel. And heard the scream of a woman – his girlfriend? – as she shoved her way through the crowd. I looked back at him. A broken nose, I thought, that's all. I'd seen worse on a rugby pitch.

So why was I shaking?

My mates had turned around. Mick had his arms around me now, pulling me away from the crime scene.

'Come on, mate. We can sort this.'

But nothing would silence the voice in my head telling me the game was over. The landlord's face said it clearly enough. The matey smile had fallen away. He couldn't help me on this. What, really? Some newcomer could shove me and my life out of the way, and help himself to what was mine?

Brian walked over. 'You're both barred,' he said, putting his hand on my shoulder, like I sometimes did when I was arresting someone I felt sorry for.

'Steve, my hands are tied,' he said. 'I could lose my licence if anyone reports a violent incident. There's TripAdvisor and social media to think of. It's all different these days.'

I stared at him, slack jawed. 'For Christ's sake, look at him!' Brian was almost shouting now. 'Do you think he's some kind of hardened criminal? He's a geeky student type, like the rest of them here. They haven't a clue how to behave in a pub. That's why I like having you here. And you've let me down. What's wrong with you?'

I looked down at the floor. Brian gave Mick a nod.

'I'll take you home, mate,' Mick said.

As he led me away, I realised that all I wanted was normal. Normal me. And normal Lois. Solving problems was what we did best. This time, I'd pick up all the clues. I'd pay attention and I'd listen. No more surprises. Next time I went out, and God knows when that would be, I'd get home early and Lois would be there, House & Garden on her lap and a glass of Pinot on the side table.

Perso e Trovato
S.L. Jones

Emanuele Roderick was pulling his belt through his trouser loops while he decided which 'work shirt' to wear today. He was looking out of the window of his street side apartment as the girl he met last night seemed to be stirring. Well, he knew he could hardly call this an apartment. This was a hotel room. A Wetherspoon's hotel room.

He was looking across the street and up to the top of the hill to the right. At a different venue. His venue. If the renovation bid was accepted by the Council. The previous owner had eagerly taken his money, but it was a heritage building so that wasn't enough to take it over. He had placed an offer on an old bank that had fallen into disuse of its original purpose decades ago. It had been a restaurant with a bar once or twice in the past few years, but each time something had gone very unfortunate for the business owner.

This was nothing to do with him of course, it was purely by chance that he had fallen upon this new business opportunity a couple of months ago. And if his bid was finally accepted, he intended for it to be more of a bar with a restaurant than a restaurant with a bar. He hadn't settled on the name yet, but it would have to be something Latin, for the Roman décor, and his heritage. But it would be a hell of a lot more magnificent than the Spoon's hotel he was currently occupying.

'Morning bab,' said the girl on the bed behind him. He shuddered inwardly at the colloquial expression. Perhaps even slightly outwardly but he hoped that hadn't been noticed.

'Hey, you. Good morning,' he turned and forced a smile at her.

Shit. She was a lot older than he remembered her being last night. She could hardly be called a girl. She, okay, yes, her body was still pretty tight, he noticed as she sat up onto her knees and let the quilt fall just enough to reveal her tits.

Hmm, pink nipples, he thought to himself. Hadn't seen them in a long time. In fact, he was surprised he had managed to pull a local, white girl anyway, despite her age. It wasn't that he thought they were 'special,' or 'better' than other types of girls. Quite the opposite. He was white himself. He preferred Asians and South Americans, it was just extremely unusual as whenever he did take a liking to a white girl, he found he was rarely successful.

'How did you sleep?' she asked.

Yes, it wasn't just her body, he remembered liking now when they were chatting at the bar downstairs last night. Her dark blue eyes and natural beauty against a very sparing amount of makeup was something he found quite captivating. Now that he could see the faintest hints of grey routes under the red, brown and blond, well blended colours. Still, he could go again.

'Best sleep all week, hun,' he said smirking and moved towards her.

'Oh yeah? She asked starting to crawl across the bed towards him. 'Why was that?'

'You remember,' he said putting a knee on the bed, ready to climb up towards her.

Then his phone rang. On the windowsill.

'Fuck sake. Sorry babe, I gotta take this.'

Emanuele walked to the window again and swiped up the phone. He was pretty sure it was who he thought it was, so he waited another ring as held it. Even at this stage he didn't want to appear too keen.

'Hello, Emmi speaking.'

'Good morning Mr Roderick. It's Stephanie Barnes, from the Business and Innovations team,' said a shrewd female voice.

'Ah, hello, Ms Barnes, thank you for getting back to me. How are you?' he asked, trying to sound optimistic.

'I'm very well, thanks. So, I have some good news for you.'

'Oh, that's great,' Emmanuel interrupted.

He sensed that she smiled.

'Yes well, you'll be pleased to know, that the council has accepted your offer of three million, for the three-year lease.'

'Oh, excellent. That's great, I'm so pleased. Thank you.'

'Yes, well that's okay, we're looking forward to working with you. Now...'

'Ahh when can I start to renovate.'

'Just a moment, please, Mr Roderick.

Somebody interrupted them to speak with her on her side of the line. Emmi tried to capture what they were saying, but they were too far away from the speaker.

'Yes, sorry about that Mr Roderick, I was just posing the question. Well, my manager had shown me the checklist which we are going to have to send over to you again. We know you've completed a few things, like the insurance and the registration with HMRC and Companies House. Your business plans impressed them more than enough.'

'So, I can move in?' he asked. 'Well, you know, not move in obviously but I mean can I get the keys? Can I start to renovate?'

'Err, yes. Yes, everything looks in order for that. You just can't start trading yet obviously.'

'Oh, okay, no, that's not a problem. I wasn't planning to just yet, as I said in a previous plan, I was expecting that to be next month anyway.'

'Okay, very well. Thank you very much for waiting patiently with us, Mr Roderick, I know how eager you were to get going,' she said. Emmi wondered if she was slightly flirting with him, but it didn't matter now. Time to make his new dreams come true.

'Brilliant. Thanks again Stephanie. I'll let you all know again once its ready and I get all the food and drink and staff and stuff to start trading. Will there be any more forms?'

'No more forms, you'll be pleased to know. We'll do one more inspection once you've finished the renovations and then I believe HMRC will send you a final letter of permission to start trading. I wish you the best of luck and can't wait to be one of the first to try that Amatriciana bucatini,' she finished with a giggle.

'Which one was.... Oh yeah, of course, yeah, I Know the one,' he said racking his brains for all the dishes he googled.

His mother's recipes were nothing like that from what he could remember, and she never really named them, when she did it was usually something very self-explanatory.

'Thanks for all your hard work Stephanie, look forward to welcoming you to Perso e Trovato!' There it was, he thought of the name. He was fairly confident translating the name of the previous establishment into Italian wouldn't result in a law suit. He hung up. Breathed in the air from the street on the steep hill bellow.

He was expecting to turn to find the girl from last night pining for him after her likely eavesdropping, but to his surprise she wasn't. She was smiling at her phone. He wondered if she was responding to some competition from internet dating or something. Maybe she wasn't even single. Did he ask her last night? He couldn't remember discussing it. Emanuele forced a small fake cough to draw her attention. She didn't look up. Perhaps the moment had passed and he wouldn't finish his pleasant start to the morning. Never mind, he'd have plenty of opportunities when he opened his new business. He went back to the mirror and thought he'd spend a couple more minutes deciding on a tie or no tie before leaving.

'Erm, excuse me. Mr. Where do you think you're going? Got somewhere to be?'

Too late now, bitch, he thought.

'Yeah, sorry, that call, it was the council. The bids been accepted.'

'Oh, well done, bab,' she said, but the enthusiasm felt forced to him.

'So, I'm off to the get the keys now and then I'll finally get to spend some time in the place alone without being watched all time by a heritage officer from the council,' Emmie said grinning at the girl.

'I don't know what time we have to check out by the way, I presumed you knew the place better than me so I'm just gonna go down now and let them know you'll hand in the key, alright?'

She scowled at him and sat up to look for her clothes.

'Whatever, dude. I got places to be too you know.'

'Alright, well that's great.' He collected his wallet and tobacco pouch from the side cabinet on her side of the bed. Her side, he thought to himself smiling. They hardly knew each other. When he got to the door he turned around and watched her looking for her things for a second.

'Say, what was your name again? Do you want to like, I dunno, trade numbers or something? I think I'll be living here for a while now.'

She looked up at him and her face betrayed complete disbelief.

'Oh, just fuck off, will you.'

He raised his eyebrows and walked out the door.

'Okay, see ya,' he muttered.

Checking out of the Wetherspoon's hotel proved to be simple task. They seemed to be busy, no questions were asked. They knew to expect one more person down soon to hand in the key.

Emanuele could have just gone out through the door opposite the reception area then, but he remembered from last night that the door on the right would take him back into the pub area. That was what he wanted. He could smell the smell of stale, spilled beer and watch all the peasant in here at that time eating their breakfast. He was half tempted to even join them and get a small one himself. The keyholder could wait around out the front of his new bar as long has he decided he realised, smirking to himself.

The lights were too bright for a pub. You could only hear the smallest murmur from people on tables. Christ, it was a weekday and term time, but there were even a couple of families eating and drinking in here at this time. Birmingham... he thought to himself walking more quickly through the pub area to the doors. Do they really deserve a new establishment as fantastic and glorious as mine?

When he got to the door, he wondered whether he should roll up and check his place but then remembered it would be nicer to get a coffee first. Not from here, obviously. If he walked up the hill, he would pass through a park with a cathedral in it the locals named after the winged wildlife. There was a Phillpotts somewhere around there, and he would get a double espresso with a sausage sandwich in brown, healthy bread.

True to the form of this city, there was immediately someone sitting against the plant pot outside the Spoons asking for money to everyone passing by. He didn't pay more attention to Emmi than anyone else, thankfully for him. It was pretty easy to rush off through the pedestrians up the hill. It was on the other side of the park where the next homeless person approaching, seemed to be a bit more threatening.

There were plenty of other people walking about now to start their jobs, why would he approach me? Emmi thought to himself hopefully. No, he was definitely coming this way. Damn it. Emmi had always pondered on what was the secret was that the homeless used to pick their targets for begging. It would almost be useful to get inside their heads, if indeed unpleasant.

'Excuse me, have you got any spare change mate? Twenty p towards my bus fair, come on.'

Twenty p, what kind of fucking peasant request was that? Did he think that if he went in small for everybody it would be quicker to build up the amount of money that he actually needed?

Emmi just followed his gut.

'No change, sorry,' he told the beggar.

'Oh, come on! Not even twenty p, what the hell?!'

Emmi could see him starting to get irate. There we are then. He was one of those ones. Basically, a polite and public mugger. Well, if and when he was going to give change to someone, he always tried to make sure he perceived them to be one of the ones who deserved it most. Women, young people. The ones that looked like they were quite fresh and new to the streets, but also had a genuine look of fear about them too. They were the ones who probably deserved to be helped. Emmi just kept walking.

Then when he got to the end of the park, he saw the Phillpotts. Shit. The homeless person was probably still watching him. If they saw that he went in and bought a coffee for himself now, they would know that he was not only lying about not having any spare change, but also extremely selfish and worse than the average person.

'Fuck sake,' Emmi muttered to himself. 'Why didn't I think this through and take a different route or something.'

There was a bus stop near the Phillpotts. Perhaps if he looked at the bus times for a while and played around with his phone, the homeless person would think he was somewhere else and forget about him. Then he could sneak in and sneak out. He played this charade out for a couple of minutes until he remembered he didn't have time for this shit. He had to meet the employee from the council that were handing him the key back at his new joint. Emmi shook his head and rolled his eyes. He was going in anyway.

By the time he had bought the mocha and the sandwich he had almost forgotten about the aggressive homeless man when he left the shop. Until he saw him again. Conveniently standing in the centre of the path he was taking. He almost had this knowing, satisfied smirk as if he knew he had won some kind of duel. Fuck! Emmi screamed internally. He had fifty p. That seemed like a fair ceasefire tribute. The humiliation at being caught out would have to be dealt with by some self-loathing later.

Emmi locked eyes with the homeless man, gave a fake smile that said he had just remembered something.

'Okay, okay, yes, I just found some change. My bad.'

'Oh, thanks mate, sorry, I really appreciate it,' said the homeless man who held his palm out.
As he dropped the change into his filthy hands, Emmi locked eyes with the homeless man once more, still smiling, but also glaring at the same time.
Go, on. Ask for more, I dare you. See what happens, Emmi thought to himself furiously. The homeless man just returned the smile, but he still held that knowing look of victory in his eyes. For a second, Emmi was convinced he would actually try it. Thankfully he said nothing more and then Emmi walked on.
It was a relief really, Emmi wasn't sure he'd have been able to hold back, if the homeless person did try to push at that last frayed, thread of his tether.

Emmi had long left his savage nature when he approached his club again. The sun rays beamed on the pillars and although yes, the white, grey exterior of the old bank was a little darkened from the wear and tear of the decades, it still stood regal and firm. Like the old Greece and Rome, it was probably trying to imitate.
Outside it stood a man in a cream shirt and a green shaded tie checking his phone and looking about impatiently. He had dirty blond hair, combed quite well but not flat.

'Oh, there you are Mr Roderick, I thought you would have been waiting for me, not the other way around. You've been pressing for us to hurry up the paperwork for months.'

'Hello, yeah sorry about that, just grabbing a coffee. Where's Stephanie, I thought she was handling the case?'

'Stephanie doesn't really do this kind of thing. Likes to keep business to business, you know.'
Emmi was disappointed, but perhaps he had come on to her a little too strong over the phone from time to time. It was hard to tell when you couldn't read someone's face.

'Alright, sure thing. Have you got the keys then?'

'Of course, Mr Roderick, I thought I'd give you a tour. Well it will have to be a quicker one than I would have

liked now, but there we are,' he said, raising his eyebrows.
I know what my fucking club looks like man, it's mine, Emmi thought to himself.

'Go on then. You really don't need to.'

'No, no. It's no trouble at all, don't worry,' said the council worker.

They just didn't want to let something that gave them a sense of control, go, did they? Emmi thought to himself. As his escort fiddled with the door and they walked in, he found himself trying to imagine the levels of micromanagement that you probably had to endure working in a place like theirs. Things needed to be perfect for everyone in the hospitality sector too he had found as he cut and diced his way to the top of his industry. Everything was so just on time and improvised when it was so busy.

The familiar whiff of stale alcohol that lingered around the Wetherspoons he left earlier, was still in the air. Lighter obviously, and the spilled drinks of this place's past had probably always been more diverse than cheap beer, but it was still here. There was no way for any establishment to get rid of it, he had learned the hard way long ago. Top of the line air conditioning was the first thing he would install around here though, over the next few weeks. Not just the decoration and the furniture.

The bar with that tasteful Victorian window thing at the top, took up a large rectangle to the right of the room, the ceiling was high and the thick pillars imitating marble columns. Most of the floor was a dark laminated wood, but towards the corner to the right around the top of the bar there was a patch of chequered tiles. Chairs were piled upside down on top of tables.

'Any idea why the previous owner didn't bother to take out all the furniture when they left?' Emmi asked his escort.

'I don't know. Laziness probably. Are you going to keep them or what?'

'No chance. New venue, everything else will have to be new too.'

His escort frowned.

'What about the paintings on the walls?'

Emmi looked at them. Faux Portraits of Victorian men and women, but mostly women.

'Nah, no chance. I think I'll put portraits up but they will be like Roman ones you know. Togas with tits hanging out, that kind of thing.'

His escort smirked, but it hardly hid his disapproval.

'Starting to sound like your place won't be much different to that underground bar beneath the Burlington Hotel, opposite the train station, you know.'

Emmi said nothing as they rounded the bar and walked through the doors into the kitchens. He was getting pretty pissed off at this guy.

'So was there anything in particular you actually want to show me or talk about or are you just gonna keep telling me everything I already know?' Emmi asked.

The council worker didn't reply just yet, he just busied himself looking all the cabinets and fitting spaces for storage freezers and fridges.

'Just thought I'd go through the hygiene and licensing standards and processes once more if that's alright.'

The man turned, looked at the disposable coffee cup Emmi was still holding.

'I know you're a busy man and all that,' he said with another smirk.

Fuck you. Emmi thought to himself.

'Go on then get it all out of your system,' Emmi replied.

The council worker droned on and on like he was reading somebody's house rules for the next twenty minutes as Emmi dragged himself around every room, corner and hallways of his new establishment, gritting his teeth and doing everything he could to block out everything his escort said.

They finally came back around to the main entrance again.

'Hope that summarised what you can and can't do to this place going forward.'

'Clear as a whistle,' Emmi replied.
They stared at each other for a moment. Emmi didn't care anymore if his seething rage was clear enough for the Council worker to see. He tried to memorise the face and vowed that any bouncer he eventually employed would know this man could never be let back in. If he went on nights out that was. He probably did afterwork drinks. With Stephanie, no doubt. Their building was just around the block.

'So, you gonna give me my key then or what?' Emmi asked.
The man smiled and reluctantly dipped his hands into his pocket. He coldly dropped them into Emmi's outstretched hand.

'Don't lose them, or the business, for matter,' he said turning on his heels and walking out.

'It's changed hands a lot of times,' he called out as he exited. There was something threatening about the way he said that.
Emmi was tempted to throw one of the chairs at the wall next to the door. He gave it a few moments, then followed him out and looked up and down the busy street to make sure he was gone. He couldn't see him. He walked back inside, closed both doors tightly then picked up one of the chairs and lobbed it at the wall. It didn't break or anything, just made a loud noise. And it didn't feel as good as Emmi suspected it would have done if he had done it just after the man had left.
Days went by and he employed the right tradesmen. The weeks went by, people and the press, showed more interest in his project. He ordered people about and made sure everything was perfect to his tastes. Scaffolding work became paint work and paint work turned into decorations and furniture. By the time Emmi was finally able to schedule an opening date, he'd spent more than he had spent to purchase the place in the first place. All without legal advice or guidance along the way. From a previous divorce, Emmanuele could remember how long solicitors always

took to process things and then there was always a new added surprise cost that had to be paid before it was done. No sir, no solicitors for me ever again he repeatedly told himself.

When he finally arrived at the opening week he had planned, he had become so accustomed to the unexpected enjoyment he had discovered in the preparation and the redevelopment of the heritage building, that he no longer felt the same excitement at opening as he had when he had begun.

It must have been in these last few days, he realised, when the council implemented their reclamation of their old building. In backhanded boardrooms his establishment changed hands again. When he was tired and worn down. His determination and his greed had their limits. This was becoming more of a burden than an investment.

The establishment opened during the day for the first time in over a year. The building opened its doors for the first time in over a year. Champagne was splashed but his people and he were holding back. People were allowed in. They took a flute at the door and then they stood at their tables socialising. It was a sunny day and their clothes reflected this. Emmi had employed only the most resilient and stress resistant kitchen staff he could find after a gruelling process of assessment centres days. The ones he had chosen were ready for the opening. Everything ran smoothly. A couple of the new bar staff were slightly slower, but everyone was served in less than a minute and a limit had been set on the number of free drinks people could have. He hoped to get everyone out by five at the latest, so that the new shift of staff could be successfully handed over to, to prepare for the real celebrations of the night to begin.

He never got to that point in the night. That point came but it passed him, as he had been given the hateful truth by the employees from the council who had come to co celebrate the opening.

The place was never really his to own.

He had been informed that his lease over the building would

be expiring by the end of that week.

Emmi laughed at first. It was a pretty sick joke for them to play but he would endure it. This was the last time any employee from the council would ever be able to set foot inside this place again anyway so he thought he'd let them play their games and have their fun.

It was only when the man who gave him the keys arranged a meeting in his back room and started to lay out a number of papers to discuss their takeover that Emmi started to believe himself. He sent for all the miles paperwork he had signed over the months leading up to the handover of the keys and re-read them. His head was swimming and he could barely process each word on the page. It looked nothing like the words he had read and signed, when he first bid and purchased the deeds to the place. When he looked up the broad smile across the man from the council's face was macabre, like something out of a nightmare. The pure satisfaction on his face was nothing short of horrifying.

He was obviously right.

Emmi had sunk every last penny of his money and soul into this place. He realised he had lost sight of the original plan so long ago, that it was too late to ever turn back. Now that would be gone. Those last few resources.

He was left with nothing.

Somehow, he didn't die. He was forced to survive and stalk the streets around the centre of Birmingham for a time that he no longer counted. Each morning he climbed out his new sleeping bag, beneath St Chad's rail and tram bridge viaduct looking thing on Lionel Street. He begged around Snow Hill Station up the hill near the Cathedral until he secured enough for a bottle of water.

This was usually by midday. Then he limped past the Phillpotts he bought that sausage sandwich from on the day they exchanged the keys with him. Every time he felt as anxious as he did on that day, but now it was because he feared that the homeless man, he had given change to would find him and recognise him. They were one of a kind now, and Emmi feared the homeless man would give him that same, sick and satisfied smile that the man from the council gave him once he pushed the papers of truth about his lease across the table at him.

He was going to do what he always did: Sit outside the door steps of the Wetherspoon's that looked across at the club that was supposed to be his. It still fuelled him, just looking at it, and this was an even better spot to beg from than around Snow Hill. He's usually spent most of the evening there before spending the last few hours begging around the canal where Brindley Place joined Broad Street.

This evening something spoiled this routine. A tall, handsome man, of a Mediterranean complexion like his own swung through the Wetherspoon's doors almost stepping on top of him. A girl who came out behind him giggling did notice him though.

'Oh sorry. Marco, look where you're walking will you.'

He recognised her before she recognised him, but he wished he hadn't. He knew who it was. He just couldn't remember her name. Some things never change, even if he and everything he knew had, but he could barely remember his own name these days anyway. It was the woman he had woken up with on the morning he was given his keys to Perso e Trovato. She looked at him with the most terrible look of sadness and floundered to say something.

Osaka nights
Sofia Kokolaki-Hall

The food-trolley man arrives. The Bentos look good, but every single one of them looks like it contains something that's died in it, so I say 'Arigato,' and off he goes.

What time is it at home? Too early to call, and I probably shouldn't be calling her anyway. I close my eyes, but I can't sleep. Two long hours pass while I stare at pagoda-roofed houses, power lines, streams and rice fields like a zombie – and that stunning cone in the distance that must be mount Fuji. I check the time again. It'll be nearly eight in the morning now; a decent time, for a week day. I fill my lungs, I call her. I hear her voice: 'Hi, you've reached Maria. I can't get to the phone right now. Please leave a message.' I don't leave a message, because I don't know what to say. Three minutes later, I receive her text. 'Too busy today. I'll try to call you tomorrow. Hope everything is alright with you and you're enjoying Japan.' No kisses, and she's forgotten my birthday. She never forgets birthdays. She even remembers the birthday of the kiosk man across our street, for fuck's sake. 'Prepare to collect your luggage,' the announcement warns me after an irritating chime. Everyone gets up, and so do I. The Shinkansen smoothly stops, the door opens and I arrive in Osaka, jetlagged, starving, and with my life falling apart.

I look around for my Airbnb hostess, Aki, who has insisted on meeting me at the station. In the numerous messages we exchanged, I tried to tell her that there was no need, that I could easily find the address using my phone map, but there was no changing her mind. I'm not sure it was a good idea to agree, how on earth are we supposed to find each other? But I hear my name, and a geeky-looking Japanese woman runs my way, carrying no less than a half-a-dozen Godzilla-sized shopping bags. How the hell did she recognise me? There are lots of Europeans around, and my Airbnb profile picture is a slightly-out-of-focus queen green olive in a martini glass.

    'Aki?' I say and offer my hand. She shakes it loosely,

then does a forty-five-degree bow. I copy her. She giggles; she's gone bright red.

'Sorry, sorry,' she tells me and I've no idea what she's sorry about.

We start to walk. My four-wheel spinner suitcase is a breeze to carry, so I offer to help her with some of her bags, but that seems to be a faux pas. 'Sorry, sorry,' she tells me red-faced again. I hope I haven't offended her. I ask her how her day has been so far. She tells me something in English, but I don't understand her. I hide my confusion behind a smile and give up on the chit chat. I look at her through the corner of my eye. She's younger than me, but she's dressed more like a granny: flat shoes, woolly tights, knee-length knitted dress, buttoned-up knitted cardi. And everything she has on is lilac, even the shoes. I smile again, when our eyes meet; she giggles and looks away.

We arrive at a huge block of flats. She juggles shopping bags and keys at the front door and opens it. In the lift, she covers every eventuality, fire, earthquake, tsunami, but I only half-register what she tells me. We stop at floor 6. I make a mental note. We walk around the balcony corridor to Flat 606. I make another mental note. Aki tells me she lives directly below, at flat 506. I'm really tired now, and very hungry. I'm dreaming of a shower, a cold beer, and a bowl of mushroom ramen, even if it swam in fish broth. Aki unlocks the door to my flat and slips off her shoes. It takes me forever to negotiate the laces of my boots.

'Sorry, sorry, thank you,' red-faced, she tells me.

I smile and try not to fall. We sanitise our hands with the gel she keeps in the tiny hallway. She dangles her shopping bags from her wrists, and gives me a pair of slippers. I put them on. She shows me around. Aki, in Japanese, means sparkle; no wonder the place is so sparking clean. I leave my jacket on a chair, feeling I'm already making a mess.

We fill in a surprising amount of paperwork and she asks me if it's OK to take a photo of the details on my passport.

'Sure,' I say, and hand it over to her.

She realises that I'm Greek, and gets super excited. Apparently, I'm her first ever guest from Greece. She asks me breathlessly which part.

'Athens,' I say. She claps her hands so hard her shopping bags collide; 'Acropolis?' she tells me. I laugh. 'I see it every day from my balcony,' I say. She looks like she might faint.

'It is my dream to see it too one day,' she tells me.

My stomach grumbles. I ask Aki if she knows where I can find vegetarian food in the neighbourhood. My question confuses her.

'Sorry, sorry,' she tells me.

'No problem,' I say.

She shows me the washing machine. I try to explain I won't be needing it; I've packed more than enough clean clothes. She takes me through the full operating instructions anyway, even though everything she says is printed-out, laminated, and stuck on the wall. The same happens with the cooker. I won't be doing any cooking either; this is my holiday. But I don't want to be rude, so I just wait until she's done. She asks me what time I want my towels and my sheets changed.

'Don't worry about it,' I say, 'I'm only here for three days. No change. It's better for the environment.'

She bows. 'Thank you, sorry,' she says.

I think that she's about to leave, but she remembers something. She fumbles with her bags and lays a week's worth of fresh fruit and snacks on my table.

'For you,' she says. 'That's very kind,' I say.

'Thank you, Aki. Am I pronouncing your name right?'

She giggles. 'Aki,' she corrects me.

'Aki,' I say, pretty much exactly the same way I said it before. She claps her hands. I smile, and she leaves me with another bow and another 'sorry, thank you.'

I eat one of Aki's bananas, and study some of her laminated messages on the wall. *Dear Guest. Thank you very much for your cooperation. Please don't wear your slippers outside your flat. Please find extra pillows and blankets in the wardrobe near your bed. For your safety, please do not open the door when someone knocks, or rings the doorbell. Please be careful of strangers! If someone comes and rings the doorbell persistently, please contact me ASAP.* There's about a million more notices, but I've had enough, so I stop there. I check my phone. Still no birthday wishes from Maria. I sniff into a tissue from a box in a lilac lace cover, then pull myself together. I google: vegetarian food in Osaka. There's a place called Cherry around the corner, which I like the look of. It's a bar, but it also does food. I shower, I change, I leave the flat, I lock the door.

I follow my map to the pin that I've dropped on Cherry. Five minutes later I arrive. I walk in. There's a handful of people scattered around in booths, drinking, or eating, all absorbed in their mobile phones. The woman behind the bar is too cool for school. She greets me aloofly in English. I sit on a stool, ask for a bottle of Sapporo and read the food menu. I order the meat-free gyoza, rice, and pickles. My phone beeps. It's not Maria, it's Aki. She's sent me a war and peace length list of vegetarian-friendly restaurants in Osaka. It finishes with a *thank you*, although this time there is no *sorry*. Cherry is not on her list.

The bar woman brings me my food, and watches me while I eat. She tells me something about the way I hold my chop sticks. Her English is better than Aki's, but I still don't fully understand what she's trying to tell me. She demonstrates, I copy. She gives me the thumbs up and smiles at me for the very first time. She's attractive. Should I be flirting, or am I spoken for? I tell her that I enjoyed my meal, she clears the plates, and I ask for another Sapporo. She shakes her head.

'Sake,' she tells me, like it's an order.

'Why not?' I say. She pours two glasses, one for me, one for herself.

'Kanpai,' she tells me, 'kanpai,' I say, and we drink.

Her name is Kamiko. Three sakes later and I've told her everything about my life; about my troubles, about my therapy, about Maria, about how I lost her; about how alone I am right now in the world. I'm not normally that open, but Kamiko is easy to talk to, and I have a feeling she gets me. I ask her if she likes working at Cherry, she nods and tells me that she edits films for a living, but because it's a lonely job, she keeps the evening shift at the bar, for meeting people. She talks to me about a personal project she seems very passionate about, for which she's been filming her own footage, that she boils down to the bone marrow, as she puts it, to produce a series of shorts. She shows me a clip on her phone. It's pretty out there, I don't follow the plot, but I like it.

I tell Kamiko about Aki. She smiles, like she knows the type.

'Like the film *Misery*,' she tells me, and I really wish she hadn't said that. We laugh about it. Then I tell her goodnight.

'This early?' she asks, looking disappointed. I tell her I need to sleep.

'Come back tomorrow,' she orders me, 'I'll cook you mushroom ramen. No fish in the broth.'

Back at the flat, I turn on the lights. Everything is pretty much as I left it. Except, there's a clean towel rolled up on the shelf to replace the one I used earlier. Did Aki come in while I was out to change it, when I specifically told her not to? And how on earth did she know I've had a shower, when most people have a shower in the mornings?

Then I see it; a little wrapped-up box, and an envelope with my name on it. There's a card inside; the first part of the handwritten message is *happy birthday* in Greek, and underneath it in English: *I am grateful to be able to spend such an important day of your life with you. Please always be yourself as a wonderful person. Aki.*

On the floor, under the table, I see what looks like a little lilac diary. I pick it up. It's a scrap book. It contains an alphabetical list of nationalities, some of them crossed out, with handwritten notes, such as names and dates, and golden star stickers stuck next to them, like an out-of-five review. Austrian Carina, got three stars; so did Belgian Arnaud and British Pete. Dutch Lars only got two, but French Sabine got four. What the fuck is this? I look further down the list. German Hanz and Adela got another three. Below is Greek, crossed out with a perfectly straight line; today's date, my name, and five golden stars next to it.

I freak. My feet take me straight out the door, which I shut behind me without thinking. I am still in Aki's slippers, without my phone, without a jacket, without any money on me. I run down the stairs. Out of breath, I arrive at Cherry. I furiously try the door, but it's locked. What time is it? I feel dizzy. Then I hear a latch slide, the door opens, and I see Kamiko's surprised face. I fall into her arms, shaking like a leaf. She takes me in, her voice soothes me. I tell her what happened. She brings me some sake to calm me down. I drink it in one. She smiles at me, and I already feel better. But then her face does this funny thing and goes all blurry. I hit the floor.

...

Aki and I have kept in touch, since she saved me that night. Apparently, she heard my door slam, came out to check everything was OK, and saw me running like mad into the night. What she did next was inappropriate perhaps, and she's apologised for it a thousand times; but I'm glad, because her instincts were right. She entered my flat, saw my boots, my coat, my phone, and wondered why I left without them. My passcode isn't hard to guess, it's my birthday. I should change it perhaps, but I still haven't got round to it. And if it had been anything else, Aki wouldn't have been able to work out where to find me. I didn't fully appreciate it at first, after my initial interview with the Japanese police, just how narrow my escape had been. Not until the Greek embassy guy visited me at the hospital and spelled it out to me.

Aki is coming over to Athens in September, and she will stay in the flat with me. With me and Maria.

A Full House
Lucy Smallbone

'Damn this place is savage,' I say spitting out a piece of gum and sticking it to the underside of the chain-link fence. I stare up at the house, its walls are crumbling from years of neglect and the front yard is so overgrown, it looks like a remake of 'Day of the Triffids.'

'Yeah its awesome!' says Smiley, tossing his empty can.

'You know they never found Amy Monk,' I say. 'She went in and never came out. I mean, how can a body just disappear, right?'

'They said some paedo took her. My mum wouldn't let me go out for days when the news broke.'

'Yeah, my little sister was freaked out too. She knew Amy from school.'

'Well it's not gonna stop us,' says Smiley. 'Ready to raise the stakes?'

'Yeah man, like always.'

'Dare you go up to the door and put your hand in there.'

I hesitate, eyeballing the rusty letterbox. It looks like a hungry mouth ready to chow down on my fingers. I lift a corner of fence and slide underneath. Dirt crumbles beneath my nails and brambles scratch my skin, 'Ouch, damn stupid weeds,' I curse unpicking them from my sleeves. But then the air turns foul and a nasty stink catches in the back of my throat.

'Oh man, it smells like something died.'

I stand on shaky legs and shove my hand through the slot, blanching as it chomps up my wrist, then I whip it out real quick before it decides it likes the taste of boy flesh.

'Sick,' I grin. 'Your turn.'

Smiley shrugs, 'Ok, hit me with it.'

There's a window with the words 'bite me' daubed in thick red lettering above it. The board is loose and squeaking in the gentle breeze.

'I'm raising you,' I say. 'Dare you to go through that window.'

He hacks back some phlegm and spits onto the ground, before yanking up the chain-link and easing his way through. Once he's made it, he saunters over to the window. I admire his confidence. He isn't afraid of anything and has been my wingman since primary school, when he rescued me from Billy bone-crusher's headlock because I wouldn't give up my football cards.

He yanks on the board and darkness spills out like tar. 'Damn that's rank,' he says, raising an elbow to his nose. I think he's going to back out, but then he wraps the sleeve of his hoody around his fist and punches in the remaining shards of glass. The house looks like it shudders or is that just my imagination?

He ducks preparing to go through but it's no easy feat. At fifteen years old, he is six foot two and towers above my slight five four build, even though I'm a whole year older than him. He somehow maneuvers his lanky legs up onto the sill and pauses. I watch as his eyes stretch wide and his mouth gapes, 'Fuck...' he cries, pulling at his hand as if it's stuck in gum and dives headfirst into the darkness. I smile as he thinks he's got me, but I'm not falling for his crazy stunt, so I thumb through the texts on my phone while I wait for him to resurface.

When I next look at the time, I realize its past nine and I've promised to play footy with my little sister before the day's out. I think about calling her but the screen snaps off, 'What the hell?' I grumble puzzling over the fact it was on full power just a minute ago. Without its illumination, all the shadows seem to congeal and I start to fidget.

'Hey Smiley, you done?' I cry.

There's no answer. I scuff the dirt with my trainers, frustration burning my ears.

'Come on man,' I shout. 'Quit jerking me around.'

I hug myself, shivering as the temperature drops a few degrees, but

Smiley doesn't reappear and now I feel a lick of fear. If he's hiding in there waiting to jump out, I'm gonna kill him.

I walk towards the window, my feet crunching on broken beer bottles and empty crisp packets.

'Jeez,' I cry, as the smell of rotting garbage and piss leaks out of the jagged hole and my stomach revolts at the thought of going anywhere near it.

'I swear to God if you're messing...'

I place my hand on the sill, 'Shit,' I yell as blistering pain shoots up my arm, scorching every nerve in my body. I try to yank it free but it's stuck fast, like a damn fly in flypaper. My heart thunders in my chest as my other hand becomes glued too. What is this? Why can't I get free? Images tumble out, Smiley making some joke, and my sister dressed in her football kit waiting for me to return.

I fight, kick and holler, enraged that this thing has got me, but it tightens its hold swallowing my wrist in a flash of agony. I jerk forwards, 'No,' I cry. 'Please, I don't wanna die.' My nose should hit solid wood but instead my head slips through an invisible barrier, exploding with pain as it begins to saw through my skull. A moment later I'm floating, and my brain is being controlled by something else. Am I dead? Surely if I were dead, I wouldn't be able to think. Something tugs at me, like a puppeteer testing its strings and I realize I'm not alone. I can sense Smiley; he's trapped here too and our minds are linked to something greater than ourselves. I try to reach out to him, 'Smiley, can you hear me?' But all I get back is static. This isn't real, it's some joke. I have to get out. I'm fighting but I only seem to hit empty air.

I try to cry but I have no tears. I can hear the scratching of dead leaves in my ears and my skin itches as if a thousand beetles are burrowing underneath. I'm feeling everything that the house is feeling, but that's impossible, how can a house be alive? I feel it opening up to me and I'm shocked to learn this house has a host, a secret planetary invader. Just like a hermit crab, the alien critter has snuck in, and made this house its home. I'm flooded with images of its past. A spaceship crashes to earth during WW2; nobody suspects, as there are bombs exploding all around. It crawls from the wreckage and buries itself under the only thing still left standing, this house. Over several weeks it squeezes its body into each tiny crevice, stretching, tearing itself thin, until it ceases to be an alien and becomes house.

Suddenly, I'm disturbed by a tremor. I'm drawn to it like an earthworm sensing rain. It sends thrills of excitement whizzing through me and I'm confused for a minute. Why do I feel like this? Then I hear them.

> 'Hey Morley, what you looking at girl?'

> 'Come look at this.'

My stomach blazes with hunger. Two kids have entered the yard and I can barely contain myself.

> 'That window's broke,' says Morley. 'I can crawl through?'

> 'Bite me!' chuckles the other, as she reads the graffiti.

> 'Ha-ha,' says Morley.

> 'You sure he hid the rucksack in there?' says the second.

> 'Yep, his idea of a joke. Thinks I'm too chicken!'

'Well I wouldn't wanna go in there. It stinks.'

'Probably just the drains,' says Morley. 'Oh look, I think I see it.'

'Go on then,' says the other girl. 'I'll wait here.'

'Stop,' I cry with a voice that's whiny, thin and definitely not my own.

'You hear that?'

'Hear what?'

'The creaking. It's like the house is talking to us.'

'It's probably just the wind,' says Morley. 'I'll be back in a minute.'

She hops up onto the sill and I swell with toxic hate. She shrieks and wriggles like a maggot on a hook. 'What the fuck...' I cry out of a non-existent mouth. Her spine pops and her bones snap. I hear the hollow crunch in my ears. Then I feel her blood ooze down my throat, its warm and salty. Some twisted part of me enjoys the taste.

'Jeez, I'm coming,' cries her friend.

'No,' I squeal. 'Stay back.'

She hesitates.

'Hang tight Morley, I'll go for help.'

I breathe out or at least imagine I breathe out, but I can't really feel much of anything accept an all-consuming hunger. Morley is trapped here with me. She is confused and in pain. I can't stand it any longer. I won't let anyone else suffer.

'You hear me you alien freak?' I shout. 'No one else is going to die.' I try to shake it but I feel it clamp down on my brain like a limpet, diluting my thoughts.

Blue lights flash, wheels rumble and the dry rattling hum of an engine draws near. I want to cover my ears but I can't. It cuts out, a door slams and feet kick up gravel.

'This is officer Lloyd at the old Swathe house. Everything looks normal.'

'Copy that,' says a muted voice at the end of a crackly line.

A phone rings; the policeman answers it. 'Oh hello princess,' he says, his voice carrying across the still evening air. 'Wow! You've made fairy cakes...have you been baking all day? Mmmmm...they smell delicious. Yes sweetheart, daddy will be home shortly. Kiss, kiss...'

The phone snaps off. 'Damn signal,' says the policeman.

He lifts the chain-link and then curses as my chewing gum gets stuck to his hand. He huffs and puffs, as he struggles to get underneath. Then he's through and I can hear the crunching of glass as he approaches. My body aches with hunger; it listens to the thud of his heart and smells the sweat on his skin. He shines a light into the downstairs window. 'Damn strange...' he mutters to himself.

'Hey kid,' he shouts. 'Get over here.'

A second pair of feet approach, they are lighter and quieter.

'Wait there...don't come any closer,' says the officer. 'You said she went through that window?'

'Yes sir, she was there one minute and then she was gone.'

'You didn't see anyone else approach the house?'

'No, we were alone.'

'It's damn strange,' he says. 'I need to take a closer look.'

'Yessss, come closer,' says the phantom voice in my head.

'What was that?' says the girl.

'Huh,' says the officer.

'Can't you hear it?'

'That's just your imagination, kid. I'm going in.'

The officer hooks his leg over the sill, 'What the...' he cries, as it becomes stuck fast and he struggles to free it. I bite down. The girl screams. I snap his thighbone and drag him through the window. I see his daughter in his dying thoughts; she has blond pigtails and is smiling up at him, her cupcakes iced with pink and blue candy flowers. His final wish is to be with her.

'Why?' I scream in anger and grief. House shows me the answer.

When its owners were forced to move after rumours of an unexploded bomb, it was content to be left alone until kids showed up with knives and spray paints. They ripped up its floors, painted vulgar words on its walls; smeared shit and pissed in the corners. They polluted its air with drugs and sex noises. After years of abuse it wanted to take back what was taken from it and so it plucks humans off the street.

I realize I'm one of those kids. I feel guilty because I have mistreated it, but it doesn't make killing me any more acceptable. 'It doesn't make it right,' I cry. 'I had a life, Smiley too and Morley. Hell, Officer Lloyd was just doing his job.'

The next morning men arrive in suits that rustle, armed with tape and flashing cameras. There is a film crew and they dismantle the fence scrabbling for the best views in a flurry of feet. There are vehicles grinding, growling and rumbling. Police tread down the garden for clues. The noise is driving me mad. Then one day it stops and solid fences are erected around the perimeter. I hear two men talking outside.

'You all right, Burt?' says the one. 'I hear this old place is up for demolition.'

'Yep, I think the council has had enough, you know given its reputation and all.'

I'm relieved there will be no more killing. The critter does not fully understand the word 'demolition,' but it suspects something as it roots around inside my head. The others, trapped here with me, have gone silent over the last few days. They sense it too.

On the day the bulldozers arrive, the alien creature starts to get jumpy. It suspects foul play and it searches for answers. I play dumb, along with my fellow captives, who seem to have accepted their fate in the belief they will finally be free of it.

The noise starts up and the machines begin tearing up the soil, uprooting trees and tossing rubbish. The alien makes a final assault in my head, prizing me open until I can no longer keep the secret. Now it knows its fate, it begins to groan and rock on its foundations. Fear trembles through it like floodwater, filling every nook and cranny, but something keeps it here. It has been changed by its greed, so twisted and broken by hate; it can longer survive on its own. It needs our harvested brains to keep it alive. It attempts to strengthen its bonds, tugging on each brain stem in turn, like a spider tugs on silk. I urge all my friends to let go of their earthly ties, to offer themselves to the light and then we can eject this son of a bitch once and for all. The threads unravel and the strands break. It squeals, shudders, quakes and creaks. The noises are so loud that the digging stops and the builders look on in silence. We overwhelm it and after years of hiding, it finally rips free, shooting underground, where without us, it will surely shrivel and die. We are snuffed out, as a brain can't survive without a body. But as the light winks out and the silence rolls in, there is just enough time to finally find some peace.

Children of the Valley
David Croser

Lachlan's day went from bad to worse when his return flight was diverted from Glasgow to Cardiff, Wales. It had begun badly when he arrived late at the airport in Las Vegas hot and tired and forty bucks poorer (not counting his losses in the casinos) having to book a taxi rather than the transfer coach he'd missed. What compounded it was the phone call from his boss.

For his boss to call at all while he was on leave was ominous enough. That it was a little after three in the afternoon Vegas time when he rang, and the plane home was boarding made it worse. Back in Glasgow that made it eleven at night.

'What? The Anderson account? What about it?' he said, cradling his phone against his shoulder while hoiking his hand luggage and fumbling his boarding card and passport to the flight attendant at the same time.

'Sir. If you could –'

'It can't be. The deal was closed out before I went on leave, they can't just – '

The flight attendant coughed.

'Sir, I'm sorry but all phones should be on flight mode before you –'

Lachlan shifted his stance to move forward and the phone slipped from his shoulder and clattered to the floor. He swore and snatched it up, ignoring the flight attendant and the queue behind him.

'Tender queries? They didn't say anything when I – what? Alright, I'll log on as soon as I get home and have a look, and –'

'Sir. Please turn off your phone.'

'I'll sort it. Yes, by five. Yes, I will. I'll ring you as soon as it's done. Yes. Understood. Bye.'

Lachlan ended the call and swore.

'Sir, would you mind –'

'What?' said Lachlan, acknowledging the flight attendant's presence at last.

'You're holding up the line.'

Lachlan glanced behind, ignoring the tired and impatient faces.

'Well, give me my bloody passport and boarding card and I'll get on the damned plane,' he said, snatching them back from the flight attendant.

'Have a good flight, sir. And please do remember to put your phone on flight mode.'

Lachlan made a show of turning off his phone and clattered off down the steps to the flight.

Ten hours and eight time zones later Lachlan stood by the baggage carousel in Cardiff, Wales airport. He'd barely slept on the flight. He really shouldn't have snuck into the toilets and done a couple of lines, but he was so wired at the thought of losing the Anderson account staying awake seemed the best option at the time. Just when things seem to be okay and the flight was nearly over and he was beginning to feel calm (*plenty of time to sort out the Anderson deal no problem easy piece of piss no worries*) news came over the PA about trouble with one of the engines. The flight would unfortunately have to divert. The pilot's voice had been calm and reassuring and ensured them everything else was just fine. People muttered and fretted, plenty of questions and not a few groans, which the cabin crew were at pains to address. Only one guy really lost it, shouting and swearing and calling the airline all kinds of useless pieces of shit and sons of bitches. In the end he had to be forcibly moved to a seat away from the other passengers and spoken to firmly by one of the co-pilots and a serious faced man who made a point of telling the irate passenger he was a US Marshall and if he didn't shut the hell up, he'd make it his business that the selfish bastard was arrested at gunpoint just as soon they touched down. That shut the man up, and he spent the last hour before touchdown sitting *real* quiet. That the irate passenger was Lachlan himself only seemed to kick in with the realisation that, should the US Marshall follow up on his promise and his hand luggage were searched, then the Anderson deal would become the least of his worries.

By the time they landed into the drizzle of a Welsh morning the coke was wearing off, and now it was only his anger and self-preservation that was keeping him going. He stared at the conveyor belt instead. If sheer frustration and impatience could make it move faster the thing would be firing cases off it like projectiles. No such luck. His phone was now so very helpfully telling him the time difference between Las Vegas and the UK, and it was nearly half eleven on a Friday morning already. Six hours left to get things sorted. Options. Options. Lachlan scrolled through his phone, stabbing at the screen. Next flight from here to Glasgow wouldn't be till three at least. Train? No chance. There - hire car! Couple of companies at the airport. Too long a drive.

As Lachlan's case finally appeared and he grabbed it and hurried through Arrivals his mind was racing. Was there a company office in Cardiff? Somewhere he could log onto the company intranet, access accounts. Couldn't be done from any computer, had to be in a company office, or...

In the middle of the Arrivals concourse Lachlan stopped, making people behind him stop and curse. He ignored them, staring at his phone. There: no office but one of their subsidiaries - a factory, not far outside of Cardiff, and a phone number. He stabbed at it, and headed for the Hertz desk.

The factory was in a place called Cwmyranghenfil. Lachlan made a couple of attempts to put this into the satnav, then gave up. Fortunately, there was a postcode, so just after midday he was gunning down the M4 towards Cardiff. The satnav directed him off the motorway onto a dual carriageway heading north, into a country of sharply wooded grey hills, which became progressively steeper and higher the further he went. It reminded him of the countryside north of Glasgow: same grey mountains, same pine forests. And bleaker. What was different here were the villages, strung out in rows of terraces hunched close against the mountainsides, glimpsed through sheets of rain, fogging up the car windows.

Approaching Merthyr Tydfil, the satnav directed him off through Pentrebach, higher and steeper. On one side a view down, down onto grey houses strung out along the valley below, on the other; dry-stone walls and empty hillsides. He passed through villages, little more than bleak blurs with names as harsh and guttural as their rows of grey, pebble dashed houses, a chapel, an off licence: Ysgwyddgwyn, Fochriw, Abertisswg. Up and up, the road narrower and narrower, twisting, flinging the car around the coiled contours of the land. Lachlan began to feel sick. Not just the relentless journey, the jetlag, coming down from the coke, but the effects of fatigue. He hadn't slept on the plane, the call from his boss churning round in his head – and now this. *How like Cumbernauld this all is. Bare unforgiving hills. Terraces of bruised, resentful houses. And the sky; the heavy, unchanging, unrelenting grey sky. I ran, I ran as far as I could, away from all this. I'm better than this. I got away. I escaped.*

And now, as the hire car went over the top of the mountainside, he looked down into a village so very like the streets and alleys he had run so very far to escape. As he passed the road sign telling him he was in Cwmyranghenfil, it felt so awfully like coming home again.

The satnav took him down the single village street. An off-license, a chapel, a miners' welfare, signs faded and peeling; plain washed-out terraces climbing up the steep sides of the valley, bleached of colour. Beyond and dwarfing the village, the sides of the valley were thickly wooded; not the neat dark ranks of coniferous plantation he'd seen and was familiar with from Scotland, but darker, thicker more irregular forest.

The wild wood.

He was not sure where that thought had come from, and turned his attention back to the village. Very few people about. Lachlan frowned. In fact, no-one at all. No adults, at least. Plenty of children, playing in the street or on bikes or standing in doorways. Shouldn't they be at school, he thought idly. Glancing in the rear-view mirror he noticed their eyes following as he passed. *Don't get many strangerrrrz round 'ere,* he thought with a smile, mentally putting on a West Country accent.

As he turned off and the gates of the factory reared into view, Lachlan was determined to stay only long enough to use the company database and get the hell out this place. It might be only forty minutes from Cardiff. It might as well be forty years. Do what needs getting done then back to the airport and a flight back to Glasgow. *And if I can't get a flight tonight then at the very least a decent hotel with satellite TV, wifi and maybe even an escort service who does visits in. Yes, some smart classy expensive hooker and who he could share a line or two with to make me forget this arsehole of a –*

He should have been paying more attention, should have slowed right down as he came through the factory gates. Instead his foot slammed on the brake and he swerved to avoid the line of children being escorted across the car park. He swore as the car juddered to a halt. If it wasn't for the seatbelt he would have gone through the windscreen. For a moment he sat there, head spinning, breath harsh and heavy. He blinked, pulled off the belt and clambered out. In spite of the drizzle and the steady wind he stood, hands on his knees, getting his breath back.

    'Are you alright?' said a voice.

Lachlan stood upright and looked at an anxious looking middle-aged woman. The children were clustered behind her; their teacher, no doubt.

    'Yes, I. What the hell are you -?' said Lachlan.

    'You nearly hit us.'

The teacher glanced behind her.

'You could have killed us,' said one of the children.

Lachlan looked past the teacher. It was a little girl, a little blonde. Eight, maybe nine.

'You hurt my arm,' said the girl.

Lachlan looked back at the teacher.

'You need to take more care, taking kids across a car park.'

'Well, I - ' she flustered.

Lachlan turned away, and grabbed his hand luggage from the car and glanced around the car park, seeing a sign for the administration block. He took a step towards it but the little girl who had spoken to him blocked his way.

'You hurt my arm,' she repeated.

The teacher moved towards her.

'Now, Ffion, I'm sure the gentleman didn't mean to - '

The little girl stared up at Lachlan.

'You hurt me.'

Lachlan stepped round her.

'You hurt me. You *hurt* me.'

Lachlan glanced back at the teacher. The middle-aged woman moved towards the little girl, who stared at her. The teacher stopped. The other children were clustered around her. Little Ffion glanced at them and they all looked up at the teacher. The teacher rubbed her mouth with the back of her hand. Lachlan sighed. Bloody teachers. Shouldn't be in charge of children if they couldn't control them. He walked towards the admin block. Only when he got to the door did he glance back.

The children were still clustered in the middle of the car park. They were all staring at him, and pointing. Lachlan frowned. No. Each child was making a fist at him with their left hands, index and little fingers pointing at him. Behind them the teacher was glancing away, wringing her hands. Lachlan snorted and went inside.

Although they were expecting him, as Lachlan had thought to ring ahead, the factory's administration block was run down and understaffed. Even before someone told him, he suspected the reason. He was taken upstairs, past empty offices and scruffy, neglected work areas. There were people about, but there was an unhurried, disconsolate air about the place. What real work was happening seemed to consist of people packing stuff away.

'We close down at the end of the month,' said the woman accompanying him.

'The factory's been limping along for years. The plug got pulled last month. Not profitable enough. No future in actually making things anymore.' At this the woman glanced at him. 'This okay?'

She showed him into a bare room with a long table and chipped, pine-clad walls. There were lighter patches here and there where pictures must have been, and a dusty venetian blind with broken slats, sagging down at one end. The drizzle had cleared and weak October sun sallowed dust motes in the heavy air. The only remotely modern looking thing was a company laptop, all set up and ready for him. Lachlan glanced at his watch. Just after half-two.

'Fine. Thanks.'

Lachlan dumped his bag by the door and sat down. He suppressed a yawn. A lot to do before five.

'Any chance of a pot of coffee?' he asked.

The woman shrugged. 'There's a kettle downstairs. I'll bring it up for you.'

She went to go.

'If you're closing down, why were there kids and a teacher in the car park just now?' Lachlan asked.

The woman shrugged again, something for which her bony frame seemed amply suited.

'School party, I suppose. We get a lot of them. Kids up here don't get to see much actual work getting done. Lots of unemployment, few prospects. Isolated. Only the one road in an out,' she said, shaking her head.

Lachlan glanced up at her. Part of him was screaming at her to fuck off and leave him to get on with some real work, work that *really* mattered, but there was another part of him whispering *you're here, you've got plenty of time;* the same part that kept him trying his luck at the tables in Vegas again and again and again, *just one more go, one more time,* until a three grand loss became a ten grand loss, then fifteen. Then seventeen. *I don't have seventeen thousand* a tiny voice whispered. Then another reminded him where the seventeen grand had come from, and if he didn't deal with the Anderson deal then the insider trading he'd done on their shares to get it would become all too apparent. *So. Only a couple of hours till five? Plenty of time.* Lachlan rubbed a hand across his brow and somehow smiled at the woman.

'You're not local?' he asked.

'Caerphilly. Management and admin; none of us from here. Factory floor, that's where you'll find any of the locals, and not many of them, either. Mostly agency staff on zero-hours contracts - 'least for the next couple of weeks and the last of the orders gets finished. Then - '

Another shrug.

'They built this place on the site of the old pit. New jobs, new industry for the valleys, we were all told. Bright new future. That was then. Place like this, only thing keeping these communities alive. Kids grow up and move away if they want to get on.'

'Not here, by the look of it,' said Lachlan. He mentioned the children he had seen on the way in. So few adults.

The woman looked away, and glanced out of the window. It was clouding over again.

'Getting dark soon.'

It didn't take long to see where the problem with the Anderson deal was (and to cover his own tracks on the insider dealing), despite the sluggish connection to the company intranet. Connection in the literal sense. No wifi. An actual old school ethernet cable dribbled across the desk and plugged into a nicotined socket in the wall. On the floor next to it the woman had plugged the duly filled kettle with a couple of cups, a crumpled bag of sugar and a jar of Nescafe on a tin tray. There was even a packet of custard creams.

Lachlan worked steadily, going through each of the tender queries, responding, closing each off and emailing responses back to the client, making sure to copy in his boss. Though he was loath to admit it, his boss had been right to ring him. He had conducted much of the negotiations with Anderson's so was in the best position to resolve any outstanding issues himself. That personal touch. Clients appreciated it.

It also meant of course should things go tits up then responsibility and accountability and all its consequences led right back to him. Fuck this up and he was out.

Lachlan was good but there were plenty of others only too keen to show how much better they could be. And then? For a moment Cumbernauld flashed across his vision, unbidden but always there, ready to prick his bubble belief. The penthouse in Glasgow's West End, the Merc, the perks; re-mortgaged to finance the gambling or monthly repayments, were all dependant on the salary, the bonuses, the regular pay stream, one pay cheque away from oblivion. Lachlan paused, and, not for the first time, reminded himself that between penthouse and pavement, there was only a fall. And the greater part of him thrilled again at the risk, the gamble, the stakes. In the gathering darkness he carried on.

How and when he came to have fallen asleep, Lachlan was unsure. He clearly remembered closing off the last of the tender queries and emailing off. The company's IT system confirmed that all issues were now resolved and he'd emailed this to his boss, to which he'd had an acknowledgement – and congratulations. Yes, he made sure he got that. Then he remembered sitting back in the chair. It had gone five and outside it was dark. He'd looked up at the ceiling, at the pockmarked polystyrene tiles where, no doubt, Christmas decorations had been tacked up and pulled down over the years and glasses of cheap bubbly clinked by the Board. Jaundiced strip lights made the ceiling a sagging moonscape. He remembered yawning, reflecting how so very tired he felt, how he hadn't slept since Las Vegas, how exhausting the journey would be back to the airport, but how very much he wanted to get away from this place. Maybe close my eyes for a little while, worth the risk. Only just after five. No sensing taking the risk too far, taking these roads half asleep. Now he was suddenly wide awake. He sat up with a start and stared at his watch.

'Christ.'

Half past nine. The laptop on front of him had gone into sleep mode and the screen was blank. The lights were on, but he could see those in the corridor were off. By his hand was a half-drunk cup of coffee. He felt the side. Cold. He shivered. Place was cold too. He took his coat off the back of the chair and shrugged into it, getting up and going into the corridor.

'Hello?'

He flicked a switch and the strip lights buzzed and stuttered on. In a way it made the emptiness of the corridor worse, emphasising how very bare it was. Like the boardroom there were patches on the walls and imprints in the carpet where charts and pictures and furniture had once been. Stripped bare. He glanced into other rooms. All empty. Tried a few doors. Locked. He swore under his breath and went to the doors at the end of the corridor. Locked. He banged it with his fists and shouted.

'Shit. *Shit.*'

He stood there, listening to his breathing. Other than a faint pattering of rain there was nothing else. He went back to the boardroom and grabbed his phone. No signal. He ran a hand across his mouth and went to the window, pushing aside the broken slats of the blind. The boardroom looked down into the car park. The only vehicle was his hire car, parked slanted across two spaces, just as he'd left it earlier. Through the factory gates he could see a couple of streetlights and that was it. There were houses on the street leading up to the factory. He remembered passing them, but there was not a light to be seen. No-one either to hear should he have banged on the window.

No. There – under a streetlight: a couple of kids, just standing there. Something – Lachlan frowned. The window was mottled with rain and fogged with condensation, but he could have sworn they were wearing masks of some kind. That's when he heard footsteps from below.

His first thought was to dismiss his immediate reaction on waking; that they had forgotten all about him and locked the place up for the weekend. That thought had been quickly followed by one that they *meant* to lock him in. The rational part of him dismissed this immediately, but like an unwanted guest that hadn't got the message it lingered in the back of his head. The way they'd looked at him when he came in (*resentful? suspicious? don't get many strangerrrrz round 'ere*), the way the woman who had shown him up had been polite, but there had been something else. The way that teacher had looked: *afraid.*

Afraid of what? Of who?

When he heard the footsteps below, he thought of the children, the way the schoolkids in the car park had stared at him, and the sight of the two masked figures under the streetlight. From his hand luggage he grabbed a brass ornament, a miniature of the Vegas Eiffel Tower he'd bought on impulse with the last couple of dollars left over from the tables. Not much, but better than nothing. Then the doors at the end of the corridor were unlocked.

Lachlan felt a little foolish wielding a brass ornament at the sight of an old man dressed as a security guard.

'Thought I heard something.'

'You did. Me - locked in this fucking shithole!'

The old man looked behind him.

'They didn't tell me there was anyone else here. I was told all the outsiders had - '

The old man went across to a window and peered out.

'You've got to get out before - ' he said.

Lachlan sighed. 'Give me a minute.'

He went to get his bag. When he got back to the corridor the old man was still at the window. Rather than looking directly out he stood to one side, as if concealing himself. He heard Lachlan's footsteps and waved a hand, ushering him to get down.

'What are you -?' said Lachlan, as the old man grabbed his shoulder and pushed him back against the wall.

'They're coming. They must know,' the old man muttered, and Lachlan could see the old man's hand was shaking, his knuckles white.

'Who? Look - are you going to let me out or - '

He stood up and stared out the window. In the faint light from the street, he could see figures walking casually through the gate and across the car park towards the factory. There was no effort at concealment. By their size and gait they could only be children. He couldn't be sure, but they also seemed to be masked. Yes. Each of them wore animal masks. Here was an owl, there a fox, there a hare. Even in the semi-darkness it was clear the masks were crude and home-made, things of cardboard and crayons, stuck with feathers and clumps of fur. What weren't home-made were the weapons they were carrying; carving knives, screwdrivers, hatchets, hammers.

'What the hell...?'

Down beside him the old man was moaning softly. 'They can't blame me. I didn't know, I didn't know.'

Lachlan glanced down at him.

'What? Are you going to let me out? It's just kids mucking about.'

He reached out to grab him, but the old man shrunk away and retreated back up the stairs.

'Hey. Come back, you old – '

Lachlan chased him up into the corridor he'd just left. The old man was stood in the doorway to the boardroom. He turned to Lachlan, and he could see how deadly pale the old man was, eyes wide, mouth an O.

'The light's on. They must have seen you.'

Lachlan grabbed the old man's shoulders. The old man looked at him, then back over his shoulder to the lighted room and the window.

'They saw you,' he said.

The old man struggled free but Lachlan, younger and stronger, pushed him up against the door frame.

'Give me your keys if you're so scared of a bunch of –

The old man fumbled with the key chain from his belt.

'They're not,' he said.

'Now what?' said Lachlan, grabbing the keys.

He grabbed his bag and turned to go.

'Children. Not *just* children.'

Lachlan snorted, rifling through the keys, which were all labelled.

'*Kids.* You all act like you're scared – you, that teacher. All they need's a slap and told who's – '

The old man shook his head violently.

'They're *His* children. They feed Him and He protects them. Annwyn. Keeps them, keeps them...'

Lachlan found the key he needed. He turned to go.

'Children. He keeps them children forever. Always has, so long as they feed Him,' the old man called after him.

As he ran back down the stairs Lachlan heard the old man calling after him.

'They feed Him. Annwyn. *They feed Him.*'

The key Lachlan had selected was labelled *Side Door.* Sure enough, some looking around on the ground floor found it. He could have chosen the main doors but - but whatever had seemed slightly odd about this place in the daylight; all the children, the absence of adults other than in the factory, the way the schoolchildren had reacted to him, and the fear – yes, that was it, the fear on the teacher's face, the way they had surrounded her, made him look for a less direct way out of the building.

The old man's raving aside, there was something very wrong here. As he hurried through the ground floor, he kept glancing. At ground level he could see the children in the car park close to: their animal masks, the way they just stood there staring at the factory, weapons and eyes glinting in the semi darkness. Patient. Waiting. There were a lot of them, but they clustered mostly around the main entrance. Only one or two round the side.

Lachlan peered through the window by the side door, to where his car was parked, barely twenty feet away. Over his shoulder was his bag and in his free hand the ornament from Vegas. *A quick run, knock those couple of nearby kids out the way if they come too close and I'm home and dry. No worries, no problem.*

He glanced down at his hand and saw it was shaking as it carefully, oh so carefully, turned the key in the lock. He felt a chill creep into his flesh.

Here's a thought, Lach. This charming little village up in the valleys, so isolated, so cut off. You know all about places like this, like back home in Cumbernauld, where nothing changes and time curdles and you either escape or choose to stay and moulder away to the end of your days. Maybe here - don't laugh - but somehow everything really does never change, and all the little children never grow up, like Never-Never-land. And it's because - you'll love this - they sacrifice all the adults to some awful Celtic god to keep them just the same. But how could such a thing be kept secret? How could it go on? Maybe they keep a few tame grownups, like frightened cattle, to look after them, do all the stuff to keep the place going (the school, the shops, the factory) but any strangerzzzz, who stray in or get their back up, maybe they're sacrificed: to Him. To keep them looking so very young, forever and ever and ever.

Lachlan licked his lips, which felt dry, as the tumbrels in the lock turned over. Gently, ever so gently, he eased the door open a crack. Just enough to peer out and check. Good. The couple of kids close by were looking the other way.

He threw open the door and ran toward the car. He made it without the children seeing him and only then, close to, did he see the slashed tyres, the broken windows.

'Fuck.'

The word wasn't loud, but loud enough for the nearest children to hear, and they turned. The others too, partially hidden by the angle of the building, turned. Some of them nudged each other and pointed, and under their masks, smiled the sweet smiles of children. As one they streamed across the car park towards him. They converged on the Merc. The knives and screwdrivers and hatchets and chunks of pipe were raised in their little hands.

'You hurt me,' they said. 'You hurt me.'

When Lachlan came to, he realised three things. Firstly, his head and body were bloody and sore. The children's attack had been so quick, so silent, they had beaten him to the ground before he had a chance to retaliate. He dimly remembered a blow to the back of his head, then nothing. Secondly, although it was still night, there was a flickering glow ahead of him. He turned his head, squinting. He was in a wild, open space. As his vision focussed, he realised it was a clearing in a forest. Branches, black and full, swayed against a wondrous sky full of stars. Dimly, he glimpsed the lights of the village glimmering in the valley below. Close by he felt the heat of a fire; a bonfire so close he could feel its heat, and his face plastered with sweat.

Around the clearing, in the light of the fire, the children stood all around him, watching. Beneath their masks, their eyes glittered.

Thirdly, he realised he was trussed and bound to a stake in the ground. However much he struggled, he couldn't move, even when he saw the other stakes, arranged in concentric rings around him. He couldn't scream. His mouth had been stuffed with something to stop him.

To his left, was a skeleton trussed to a stake, rags of clothing fluttering in the breeze. And another, And another. And another. They all seemed to be grinning. As he whipped his head from side to side, he couldn't help notice the peculiar state of the bones. Some of them were badly scattered about their stakes, and a few seemed oddly *dissolved* at the ends, with suggestions of charring. Each lolling skull had a gaping hole in the top, as if something had burned though.

Lachlan tried screaming again. He croaked, but no more.

That was when he heard it coming: not the children or the wind but something much larger, moving down through the ancient trees towards the clearing. Then something else: the children singing. As one they stepped back towards the edges of the clearing. Those with their backs to the forest parted, and moved to form two lines with a wide gap between them. At the end of their lines, Lachlan watched the children kneel and bow their heads.

It was coming closer now and he could hear it, pushing through the trees. He could hear it breathing, and its breath was the sigh of the wind and the forest and the valley. The trees on the far side of the clearing, beyond the light of the bonfire, had darkened, as if some giant shadow had blotted it out.

Lachlan whimpered.

Him. Annwyn. He who keeps the children forever young. He began to come into the children, and as he did the children beat their weapons on the ground, all together, like the heartbeat of some immense being.

Lachlan glimpsed something huge, blotting out the starlit sky, something with a single burning eye the size of the moon. Something that smelled like rotting leaves lying thick on the ancient forest floor. In his head, he felt a sudden terrible heat, as if the bonfire had taken hold inside his skull. He tried to scream. But he did not scream long.

Night freshened into morning.

The children of the valley had stayed there throughout the night, watching as He feasted. What was left of the outsider was not a skeleton yet, but it would be. In time; and here, deep in the valleys, in this valley, there was nothing but time; the same time keeping the children forever young. Around the valley the trees and the darkness between them and around them rustled and whispered secretly. They were well pleased.

A Cry for Change
P. V. Mroso

Nerei woke up, dressed in a hurry, took his piping hot mug of coffee and was off to the field to spend the morning weeding. Soon he was hot, sweaty and hungry. When he stood up to arch his back and mop his brow, he saw a head bobbing through the corn. He leaned on the hoe, squinted, and smiled when he realised it was Matilda.

'I brought your lunch,' she called. 'I have to go to the market.'

Nerei rushed to take the basket and rummaged through the contents.

Matilda smiled curiously and said, 'Your shirt is inside out.'

'Thanks,' he said, looking down. 'What would I do without you?'

'What is the date today?' Matilda asked.

Nerei was whistling a tune of his young days and, watching the long dancing shadows of the garden plants, he tried to recall the date.

'Happy birthday,' she sang. With a smile, Matilda presented him with a bottle of wine.

'Keep that bottle for our meal later,' he said. 'There may be a beer in the shed.'

She went into the shed, dodging tools hanging from the ceiling.

'No self-respecting man at sixty would ask his wife to enter this dirty shed,' Matilda said, as she rummaged through cartons, empty bottles and mangled beer cans.

She stepped on something smooth that was under a soiled rug close to the door. Underneath she found an old dusty bottle. It was still full and had a familiar tamper-proof seal. Nerei spotted the handwritten label and realised it was one of his best homebrew batches of experimental moonshine. He took the bottle and licked his lips with admiration.

'Thank you, my dear; this was a great year for homebrew.'

'Do you mean the stuff that knocked you out for three days?'

Nerei was silent.

Matilda added, 'Invite your two rich neighbours, but this time drink less.'

Bluebent and Redhead arrived and handed him his birthday present.

'Happy birthday Nerei,' his neighbours announced.

'Thank you, I am glad you came,' Nerei said as he placed their single bottle of cheap wine under his folding chair. They shared glasses of the recently discovered moonshine.

'You look good at sixty,' said Redhead. 'I can't believe I am sixty-five and Bluebent is seventy,' said Redhead.

The three men continued their banter until the sky was bright with stars. Then Redhead asked, 'Do farmers ever retire?'

'Farmers neither retire nor get rich, they toil until they turn into the soil they work on,' Nerei replied gnashing his teeth. He stretched to pour a drink; the bottle was empty.

'Good night,' he said as he staggered towards the shed.

Nerei was on his knees about to lie down, when he heard Matilda shriek.

'Nerei Kramba, if you think you are sleeping in this den on your birthday you must have lost your senses. Stand up, drink some milk and off to bed.'

He stood up and found he was unsteady on his feet. He drank the milk while leaning on Matilda on his way to bed. Propped up with pillows he began to relax ad drift off to sleep.

From out of nowhere, Nerei saw a small group of people appear in his room. They smiled as they looked at him curiously.

'Who are you, what are you doing here?'

A tall thin elderly man with a walking stick lumbered slowly closer to Nerei's bed and spoke softly; 'My name is Theodori Stambuli. You are our great-great-grandfather.'

'What joke is this? Is this a hospital, how did I get here?'

'Please let me explain,' Theodori spoke tenderly.

'You have been here for a long time, since the earthquake that came after the volcanic eruption of Mount Bokiboki. It spewed ash, debris and magma then crumbled into a table-shaped elevation. The massive explosion killed many people. Your swift action of moving many people to safety in a cave helped to preserve lives.'

Theodori paused to clear his throat. 'You were exhausted, and you collapsed when you realised that the survivors were very few and there was no hope of getting anyone alive. You have slept through three centuries in this state of *'in-between'.*'

'Is this a joke?' Nerei asked.

'Let us show him outside,' a deep voice suggested.

'Can he walk?' another voice asked.

'We carry him,' said the deep voice.

Nerei was standing shoulder to shoulder between two strong young men. Nerei faced west, he did not see mount Bokiboki, but an extensive scrubland, and then when he faced east and saw the emptiness without the shimmering lights of the town of Kitoki, Nerei kept silent. 'The town is now underwater; the ship sailed over it then ran aground. The hungry passengers came on land and found us,' said Theodori.

'I am hungry,' said Rufus, a very fat boy.

'It is only ten o'clock my son, wait till noon for lunch.' said his father.

One thin boy nudged another equally small and thin boy and said, 'He is lucky he gets lunch, we eat only once a day at night.' Theodori looked at Nerei, their grandfather; the short stocky man was quiet but looking at the land that had changed to a dark grey world without shadows.

'Can we travel to see more land?' asked Nerei.

'No grandfather, it is not safe to walk on this land. There are bottomless pits, and deep gorges, caused by collapsed lava tubes, that have claimed many lives.' Theodori replied.

'It is not nice, let us go inside,' said Nerei.

'Yes Grandfather,' obliged Theodori.

'Please tell him our names,' a timid schoolboy who called Theodori grandad pleaded.

Theodori put his hand on every child's head as he called the names in front of Nerei including Rufus. He ended the introduction by saying, 'These youngsters are the twelfth generation of your great-grandchildren.'

Theodori then continued telling Nerei how life had been in the last three centuries.

'Your family, in the years that followed, survived

seasons of droughts, floods, heat, cold and intermittent bouts of hurricanes, tsunamis and cyclones. More caves were excavated to accommodate the hungry people who found us. They boosted our numbers and with the exchange of knowledge of food production, our survival chances increased. Those visitors were from many far lands with different survival skills.

Theodori went on to narrate, 'Grandad, the visitors spoke of turbulent seas that boiled so much no sailing was possible and the sky was so full of debris making flying impossible. The toxic atmosphere caused by remnants of chemicals and nuclear debris from conflicts due to meagre resources put survival at its limit.'

Nerei, confused, asked, 'When am I going home?'

'You are at your home great-grandad,' answered Theodori humbly.

Then Theodori continued, 'It is a credit to you for taking action promptly to save lives in the initial disaster. We may be the only survivors on the whole planet.'

Then Theodori bowed and said, 'We thank you, great grandfather.'

Nerei asked, 'What have you been doing to survive in such a hostile world?'

'Grandad,' Theodori replied, 'Your nation has changed to respect nature to avoid the wrath of mother earth. We do not create any emissions; we capture and secure to maintain the natural balance.'

A small, slightly malnourished schoolboy moved close to the bed of Nerei and said, 'Grandad, we are not allowed to play games like football, eat apples or go swimming.'

Nerei asked Theodori to explain.

'The air does not support activities that need exertion, and for their health, we have had to make restrictions. Many fruits are poisonous and more toxic to the young. Water in ponds is polluted while rivers have unpredicted flash floods.'

Theodori bowed and said, 'I am taking this opportunity on behalf of all of us to say sorry.'

'Sorry for what?' Nerei asked

'Sorry for your loss grandad.'

'What loss?' Nerei asked.

'Your wife, our great grandmother was swept by the

torrent of water and was not found.'

'Matilda?'

'Gone,' said Theodori.

Nerei awoke in a pool of sweat, mumbling, 'No, no - '

'Was that a dream?' Matilda asked while massaging his back.

Nerei, then awake, turned to his wife and embraced her as if he had not seen her for years and then he asked, 'What happened yesterday?'

'What do you remember?' enquired Matilda

'I remember having a drink with Redhead and Bluebent and now in an embrace with you.'

Matilda slid out of the embrace to go to make breakfast.

At breakfast, Nerei's fixated on the cracking and peeling of the shell of his hard-boiled egg.

'Are you still under the influence?' Matilda asked.

Nerei promptly replied, 'No, I am as clear-headed as a farmer counting his money after an auction, I stopped drinking since yesterday.'

He stood and walked to go out. He picked an apple from his fruit-laden tree and bit into it. He rushed in and gave Matilda that apple and said, 'My dear I am worried about the future for my grandchildren.'

Matilda looked at Nerei and asked, 'Don't worry; they are healthy, in school and doing well.'

'Matilda, my dear, it is what I saw in my dream last night.'

Matilda gave him full attention as Nerei, close to tears, recounted the sequence of all the events of his dream.

Matilda said, 'I will be long gone. I won't face those horrible things.'

Nerei replied. 'Our grandchildren will be crying for change.'

When Nerei suggested seeking Bluebent and Redhead's opinion about the meaning of his dream, Matilda quickly said, 'No, those two will only laugh. Besides, they have dodgy pasts. Go to see the clever minds at the college.'

'The thought of going to a professor to claim a dream as a fact is ridiculous bordering on stupidity. 'Bluebent was formerly a professor; why not consult him first?'

The doorbell rang urgently. Matilda stopped washing up and hastily went to open the door. She saw the Bluebent and Redhead standing there, and said;

'It's a bit early for more isn't it?'

Bluebent and Redhead, sensing hostility, asked, 'Is Nerei alright?'

'Come in,' said Matilda grudgingly.

Redhead instantly asked Nerei, 'What did you put in our drink last night?'

'Why are you suddenly concerned?' said Matilda. 'You were very happy when you left last night.'

Nerei finally said calmly, 'I had a vivid dream last night.'

Bluebent said, 'I had a dream too.'

'And me too,' Redhead admitted candidly.

Then in unison, they said, 'The dreams were vivid and scary.'

Bluebent began, 'In my dream, I was going to the hospital to see a sick friend. At the closed gate, many people were intending to enter. I moved to a mound to see beyond the hospital gate. The grounds were full of people standing, sitting and lying down. Everyone was frantically scratching some part of their bodies, looking sad or crying. Posters had been hurriedly put up on the walls, with this odd message on them:

Go home, no space in the hospital. Contagious unknown microbes that cause itching and eventual death within 72 hours. We have no cure!

'The poster caused panic. People were crying, running and crashing into each other. Some stood still, frozen with fear and stepped on those who had fallen. I started to run for home, trying to avoid the contaminated ones. I saw a clear path and dashed to get through. Then an infected woman approached me for help. I dashed through some bushes but fell into a ditch. I was afraid that I was going to die. I became hysterical as I attempted to get out of that hole.'

Then Redhead began, 'I was sitting on a tall bar stool, looking at the vast sandy beach and the blue sea beyond. The bar was at a raised part of the beach near the lifeguards' station. People were swimming and splashing and playing games. Then the sea changed. Giant waves approached the beach. There was a lot of talking and shouting. Then a creature came out from the waves, an animal that looked like a giant rat with enormous teeth. It was the size of a lion I tell you, but its whole skin was covered in fish-like scales. It had a fin-like tail and ears that looked like gills with sharp-clawed webbed feet. The creature was a cross of fish, rat and lion. There was a frenzy of photo-taking by some people thinking it was docile since it stood still for a few minutes.

'Then it screeched. Out from the sea sprang thousands upon thousands of similar creatures of various sizes. They started hunting and feeding, tearing people to bits. It was carnage. I ran. Then just as quickly they disappeared, and the survivors were wondering around confused. It was a disaster zone.'

Then Nerei recounted his dream; the diffused sun, the destroyed mountain, the submerged city, the starving sailors' arrival, the barren lands, the toxic environment and the plight of the grandchildren. And worse, the loss of Matilda.
Matilda added, 'When Nerei woke up, he embraced me as the day we had our first kiss.'

'I was glad to find you because I was told in the dream you were gone,' said Nerei. He was tired, hungry and confused and added, 'Let us continue the talk tomorrow; I am tired, hungry and confused.'

The rattling noise of the letterbox forced Nerei to wake up early. It was a handwritten note pushed in.

'It's from Felista. We are invited to Bluebents house for breakfast,' he said.

'It is about time,' Matilda commented. 'They can afford it after all.'
After breakfast, at Bluebent's house, the men and women amicably agreed to discuss in separate groups.
An hour later, the three women each with a glass of white wine, approached their menfolk and sat down in silence. The three men were equally quiet.
Redhead asked, 'What did you do ladies?'
Regina, his wife, answered;
'We were looking at incurable diseases that are on the increase. We wondered whether the environmental changes, natural or human influenced, could have a contributory role.'

Regina continued to say, 'We singled out Dementia, a condition that afflicted your very own sister, Matilda. When I was a nurse, it was always considered a cruel, stigmatized, slow killer that takes all dignity from the sufferer and all energy from those who cared for them.'

Redhead snappishly said, 'There is no link whatsoever.'

'How can you be so certain?' Matilda said. 'How do you explain when you see a loved one deteriorate into a shell of their former self?'

Redhead was silent.

Matilda continued with irritation, 'You were the chief of a large group of companies with chemical crap that poisoned rivers, pumping it into the poor communities. That's what the monster in your dream represents. How do you know you didn't cause dementia to a whole generation with that filth?'

Felista said, 'Matilda you are very angry, your sister's illness may be from food, not necessarily for what they did.'

'Maybe not,' Matilda replied angrily. 'But that's no excuse for a total lack of responsibility.'

She turned her anger on Bluebent then, saying, 'You were a senior man, a professor, in the higher learning institutions and an advisor of Governments. You had funds to make things better. You spent most of it for your gratification and then biased research to support those who polluted the environment. And you failed to compensate those affected. You backed the notion that disasters were mere planet adjustments. Now you tell us about infectious diseases from the bad environment. The killer microbes in your dream were the result of your negligence.'

There was silence.

Nerei took his wife's hand. She snatched it away, saying, 'You are as guilty as these two, with all the weed killers, insecticides and fertilisers you use all over the farm.'

She stormed out and Nerei followed quietly behind her.

'I think it was your wine Felista,' Bluebent remarked.

The next morning, Nerei answered the phone to receive an invitation to breakfast at Redhead's house. He hung up and turned to Matilda. 'What is happening to these two rich skinflints? Have their dreams changed them?'

'There is the first time for everything. Let's go and see.' Matilda said as she dressed.

It was a good spread of delicious food consumed in hushed tones. At the end of breakfast Matilda stood up and said,

'I am sorry for being harsh to you the other day, not because of the wine but the thought of my suffering sister.'

Redhead stood up and humbly said, 'What you said yesterday was true. I welcome people who do not lie.'

Bluebent stood up too and said to Matilda, 'It is true you were harsh, but you spoke the truth. I know I've not acted wisely in the past.'

Nerei calmly spoke and said, 'Matilda, I am a farmer, I have to use chemicals for fertilizers, insecticides or weed killers to boost my produce for food and earn cash to survive. The work is hard, I toil, I sweat, I ache, and I drink to ease stress. They are the things a man has to do.'

Redhead looking very gloomy. He stood up and said, 'As a former CEO of a group of companies, I knew that the numerous factories emitted toxic chemicals and I did nothing. Profit tended to override all responsibilities. I dreamt about killer monsters. I was the monster who as a leader caused the death of many.'

Matilda smiled to herself.

Bluebent, nudged by his wife, stood up and said, 'My friends, before I retired, I was a professor of Environmental Sciences and was privileged to give advice. I was partial. I wrote papers to convince the public that the earth could adjust itself from any types of emissions man could produce. We were funded to do experiments to show that all the disasters were transient and would not affect life on earth significantly. The dream about mass killing microbes may have sprung from industrial effluents and I cannot avoid being blamed for not acting responsibly.'

Nerei said, 'We have to find ways of preventing our future grandchildren from the suffering which felt so real in our dreams.'

'Now that sounds professorial,' said Regina, sipping her wine.

Regina said, 'Our goal should be a cry for change to prevent what you saw in your dream, Nerei.'

Bluebent added, 'Such natural upheavals in the world caused by disasters as in Nerei's dream are random. Human carelessness for our habitat is inexcusable.'

Redhead planted his hand firmly down on the table and said, 'Let's write to the university, for Nerei to sign.'

Nerei protested, 'We are friends; I don't want all the glory. Or the blame.'

Redhead said, 'Bluebent was dishonourably discharged from the University for modifying results to favour the desired goal. In my case, I had to resign due to false accounting.'

There was silence. Bluebent cleared his throat, 'I know a young professor of Planetary Physics. I will write to him. His name is Rufus Ngalasoni-Jones.'

Nerei stood up suddenly and shouted, 'What? In my dream, one schoolboy was called Rufus. What a coincidence.'

'Not an easy man to get hold of,' said Redhead.

Bluebent said, 'We can send it to his deputy, Theodori Stambuli.'

Nerei was dumbfounded. He said, 'My friends it is as if I am dreaming again, that is the name of the eighty-year-old, my great-grandchild who was re-counting in the dream about the goings-on of his past three centuries.'

There was silence.

Matilda took her husband's arm. 'Write to both professors and don't mention dreams, she said. 'Or moonshine.'

Bluebent rummaged in a drawer and pulled out a few old scientific journals. He thumbed through one urgently and presented a picture of a smiling man in a lush garden.

'This is him,' he said.

Nerei was relieved to see that he did not resemble the Theodori of his dream. He glanced woozily over the text, entitled 'A Cry For Change'. Matilda, beside him, did the same.

'He talks about some keen observations here,' Matilda said. 'Some irreversible changes in the natural balance. The trend, he says, *when projected to the future, spells disaster for our planet.*'

Nerei moved away from the table and wandered towards the patio and the green palms outside. He thought of the centuries ahead and said, 'At least it is the truth.'

Inca Dreams
Faith Walsh

A small, stone-built hut with a thatched roof sitting at the edge of the village, away from the other buildings. The hut looks towards the terraced field that are cut into the side of the mountain, but as there are no windows the girl inside can't see the view. The gap between the walls and the roof let in air and light, so the girl knows that dawn has passed into morning. She stands by the door listening for someone to pass by, she recognises the footsteps of her sister and calls out to her.

'I'm so hungry, please give me something to eat. Anything. Please Amrita.'
'No, Huaina. You have to fast for three days. It's only the first afternoon, you can't be that hungry.'
'I'm starving. I'm going to die.'
'No, you're not. Have a drink of water. The time will soon pass, you have the feast in your honour to look forward to. Pray to Inti, our great Sun God, to guide you.'
'I can't concentrate on prayers while my stomach is making so much noise.'
'I'm going. I can't listen to you moaning any longer. I have twice the work to do as you're in seclusion.'
'It's not my fault. I'd rather be working with you than stuck here.'
'We all go through this ritual when we become women. It's a special, sacred time. I don't remember anyone else making this much fuss. I've left a jug of water outside the door.'
'Amrita, don't go.'

I call to my sister a couple more times, but I don't get a reply, I half open the door. There is a cord across the door frame so I can't open it fully, or if I did, I would break the seal. Everyone would know that I'd tried to get out and the three days would start again. Amrita has left a jug of water and a beaker. I had hoped she would have left me a maize cake or a piece of bread, but no. I take the jug inside, close the door and pour a drink of water. It does help a little, but I'm still very hungry. And I'm bored. It's all very well to be told to spend the days in quiet reflection and prayer, but you can't do that all the time, or rather I can't.

I put off telling mother that my first monthly bleed had arrived. I knew what would happen, but she noticed just as I knew she would. When I asked her why I had to fast and be kept in seclusion she replied that it was a tradition so girls could think about what it means to be a woman. I'm sure I could think about being a woman and still eat. I feel the same except that my breasts are sore, they don't seem any bigger.

Now that I'm a woman, father will start looking for a husband for me although he hasn't been successful in finding one for Amrita and she's nearly two years older than me. I thought Huaman liked her, but he married Saywa and she's expecting a baby. I don't know who I want for a husband. Amrita teases me about Huallpa. I do like him; he makes me laugh but I don't see him very often as he lives at the other end of the valley. I hope he's coming to my feast. Father would probably like me to marry Apichi as his father is the Chief Elder, but he smells and never seems to smile. There must be other suitable boys. I'm the prettiest girl in the valley according to father but he is biased. My hair is my best feature, long and glossy and when I can persuade Amrita to oil it, shines black blue like the wings of a condor. My skin is my other good feature, smooth with no blemishes. Father says that I am as pretty as any of the Chosen Women that he saw in Cusco when he went to work on a new royal palace.

Maybe I should try to pray, I kneel down and close my eyes.

'Wondrous Inti, I ask you to keep my family safe and send me a kind, good looking husband.' My stomach gives a loud rumble. 'I hope you heard my request. I know you're busy, but it would mean a lot to me and if you have the time can you find Amrita a husband too. She's too devout to ask for herself.' I wish I had an offering to make but the room is bare apart from a bed and stool.

The light is fading, it will soon be too dark to work, and people will start coming in from the fields. Mother will have a pot of stew on the fire. She and Amrita will carry on doing their sewing while they wait for father to return. The cuy will be running around as they always escape from their pen, mother will shoo them away. Father will talk what he has been doing during the day, fill in the gossip from the elders meeting or, after he has had a couple of beakers of chichi, he'll start on one of his tales of when he was working for the Inca in Cusco or serving in the army. We've heard all the stories before, but he manages to make them exciting to listen to each time.

'Huaina.'

I get up and stand by the door. 'Who is it?'

'It's us.'

I recognise Mayu's voice; she had her ceremony last year even though she's younger than me.

'Hello Mayu and I guess that Illa is with you?' Giggles confirm my guess. 'Have you brought something to eat.'

'No. It's bad luck. You only have another two days to get through. I did it.'

'Everyone keeps telling me that, but it doesn't help. What are you going to wear to my feast?'

'My blue tunic,' Illa giggles. Blue is her favourite colour and the tunic is too small for her now, but she still wears it to every festival.

'We'd best go before someone sees us. May Inti protect you.' Mayu says.

I hear the two of them laugh as they walk away. I'm so bored. I walk round the room, count to a hundred, repeat. I think I'll die of boredom before they let me out of here. I lie down on the bed and think of what I'll wear to my ceremony. I know Amrita has been working on a new belt for me although she denied it. Mother has a shawl ready for me, I overheard her talking to Aunt Cora about it a couple of months ago. I hope Father has sent a message to all the other villages nearby. It would be nice to see Huallpa again.

I try to will my condor to come to me in a dream. I call him my condor as I often dream of him. My favourite dream is the one where he picks me up and takes me soaring over the mountains to the sea. He swoops so low that the spray from the waves falls over me like a gentle rain. Huge sea creatures with blue skin leap in and out of the water. I'd like to join them, but my condor takes me up; higher and higher we fly until I think we must soon reach Inti's realm. We are close to the sun and I'm sweating, my hands are greasy and I don't think I'll be able to hold on much longer, but my condor understands and we start

to descend and he puts me down gently in the terrace field above our house. I must have fallen asleep as I'm woken by mother on her way to the fields, she calls to tell me that she's left a fresh jug of water for me. 'Be strong Huaina,' she says. 'Put your faith in Pachamama, the spirit of the earth. She will protect you.'
Today is even longer than yesterday. I picture mother and the other villagers heading to the terraced fields cut into the side of the hill, the maize is nearly ready for harvest. There will be potatoes to dig up and lay out to dry, maybe some beans to pick. Later in the afternoon Amrita brings me some water, I don't bother asking her if she's brought me anything to eat.

'Have you been praying to Inti?' she asks.

'Yes,' I reply as I finished braiding my hair. I've plaited and unplaited it about ten times. Amrita is the most pious person I know; she would make a good priestess.

'I will pray for you,' she says. 'And this time tomorrow I will be coming to get you for your blessing ceremony and feast.'

'Thank you, sister.' I reply. 'May Inti bless you.'
Who knew that a day could be so long? I promise never to moan again about having too much work to do.
Mayu calls to me on her way home. 'Not long now Huaina. Have you heard?'

'How am I supposed to hear anything shut away in here?'

'An envoy from the Inca is coming to the village to check on the storerooms and lodge house. He'll arrive the day after your feast. I thought Amrita would have told you.'

'She just told me to pray.'

'There's something else. It's just a rumour. I shouldn't tell you.'

'You have to tell me now that you've mentioned it.' Mayu can never keep a secret.

'Well, Rontu says that the elders are going to ask the envoy to accept one of us girls as a Chosen Woman.'

'Really? Can it be true? No girl from our village has ever been a Chosen Woman.' I say.

'Rontu heard her father talking about it with some of the village elders.' Rontu's father is the village administrator so she's usually reliable.

'I must go,' Mayu says. 'Wouldn't it be fun to be a Chosen Woman and go to Cusco. I shall ask mother to look out for some fine cloth to make me a new robe. May Inti bless you. See you tomorrow.'

I hope Mayu is right and an envoy is coming and the elders are going to propose a girl as a Chosen Woman. I could hear the excitement in her voice, I don't think she made it up to tease me. If she has, I'll think of a suitable punishment. Father is bound to suggest me as Chosen Woman but so will Mayu's father and Rontu's. I would love so much to go to Cusco. I close my eyes and pray to Inti. I promise to be good and to honour him and do as he wills.

'Huaina, wake up,' Amrita is shaking me. I think for a moment that I have slept through the night and day and it's time for my ceremony, but it's still dark outside.

'It's father,' she says handing me my shawl. 'He's having one of his nightmares. He's woken half the village with his shouting. Neither mother nor I can calm him, you're good with him.'

I follow Amrita and we soon find father. He's running through the village shouting and waving his arms; several people have come out to see what is going on.

'There's nothing to worry about,' Amrita says to them. 'Father's just having a bad dream. Go back to bed, we'll look after him.' Some grumble about being woken, and others stay outside to see what's going to happen next.

I catch up with Father as he's trying to get into Ussu's llama paddock.

'Father, it's late. Shall we go back home?' I ask, putting my arm on his, but he shakes it off. 'Shush.'
Father crouches down by the wall and I join him.

'Do you see those beasts?' He asks pointing at the llamas. 'Don't get too close. They are ferocious beings.'

The llamas, huddled in the far corner of the enclosure, are the least fierce beasts imaginable.

'They won't harm us,' I say.

'Are the strangers with them?'
'No,' I reply.
'Are you certain? I saw them. I think they're still here,' he says. 'Can't you see them?' He's pointing at the stone wall at the far side of the paddock. 'They are devious. Don't stand up. They've come to kill us. They have their weapons that can spit out fire. They have killed so many already. They show no mercy, their swords are sharp enough to cut off a man's head with one swipe.'

I take a deep breath. 'Yes. I see them.' I whisper.

Father is trembling, he looks right and left as if expecting someone to rush at him. He hasn't had a bad night for some time and we had hoped that his nightmares had stopped. His bad dreams always involve death and destruction and these strangers. I feel that I almost know them; they're unlike anyone in the valley. They are tall with hair covering almost all of the lower part of their faces and speak a different language. They wear armour on their bodies and ride animals which are twice the height of a llama and can outpace the fastest runner.

'They may not have noticed us,' Father says.

There's a nearly full moon in a cloudless sky. I put my hand to my ear as if straining to hear a slight sound. 'I think they're going,' I say. I get to my knees and peep over the wall, almost expecting to be confronted by a vicious stranger.

'Be careful Huaina.' Father tries to pull me down.

'We're safe now. They're going away.'

'Are you sure?'

'Yes, they're leaving the village. We can go home now. The danger has passed'

'Are you really sure that they're leaving? It may be a trick to make us show ourselves.'

'They have gone,' I say, trying to stand up, but father pulls me back down. I put my finger to my lips and slowly rise, then I signal to father to get up.

Father stands up too, he is sweating despite the cool night air. 'You're a good girl Huaina.'

I put my arm through his and lead him out of the paddock where Amrita, Mother and Ussu are waiting.

'All is well,' Father says nodding to Ussu. 'The strangers have left. You can sleep easily.'

Ussu is about to say something, but I shake my head. Father lets us take him home and mother puts him to bed.

'I'd hoped father's nightmares were over,' I say, stifling a yawn.

'Perhaps it's worry about the envoy,' Amrita says.

So, she did know but didn't tell me.

'Father has been talking to Pachacuti who believes that his dreams are visions, that Inti is trying to send a warning. He thinks that the envoy coming here is a sign that Father should speak to him about the danger.' Amrita continues.

'But why choose Father? Why not a High Priest or the Inca himself? What's the point of sending a message to a village elder?' I ask.

'I don't know,' Amrita says. 'The spirits speak to us in many ways.'

Mother comes back into the room and says that I can stay here rather than go back into seclusion. 'I'll speak to Pachacuti tomorrow and explain what has happened.'

'But, you can't have that,' Amrita says, slapping my hand as I reach for a crust of cornbread.

Father doesn't wake up again in the night and at first light mother and Amrita lead me back to the hut and reseal the cord. When the sun sets, they will come to fetch me for the purification ceremony. I try to be a dutiful girl and pray to our illustrious sun god, the almighty Inti, but my mind keeps wandering, thinking about what it would be like to be a Chosen Woman.

'Inti show me the way,' I beg, but he must be busy as he doesn't send any sort of sign.

Eventually, mother and Amrita come to take me home where they bathe me, oil my hair and dress me in a blue robe with the new belt and shawl. Father comes back from the elders meeting and he's like his old self and doesn't mention last night's event.

'Huaina, my dear daughter,' he says kissing me on the cheek. 'This is a blessed day. You are no longer a girl, but a beautiful young woman. May Inti's glory shine on you.'

We go to the temple where the priest and a few villagers are waiting for us. The priest blesses me, wishes me a long, happy life with many sons and daughters, which is nice, but I wish he would get on with the ceremony so I can get something to eat.

At last he stops talking and gives me a pouch of coco leaves that he has blessed, and we go to my uncle's house where my mother and my aunts have prepared a meal.

Finally, I get to eat.

Bowls of steaming quinoa soup, slices of dried llama meat and maize cakes are handed around. My aunts ask me how I feel and my uncle gives a speech praising me, but most of the talk is about the impending visit; what will the envoy be like, who will greet him, what he will want to do? They lower their voices when they talk about who to put forward as a Chosen Woman but I can hear father and Mayu's father. Neither of them have learned to speak quietly.

Usually a girl's coming of age ceremony carries on to the following day which is when people from the nearby villages come and there is music and dancing, but mine has been cut short because of the big visit. It means I won't get to see Huallpa for ages and it won't be my special day.

'Don't look so miserable Huaina,' she says. 'There will be another feast in a few days' time to welcome the visitors.'

'Yes, but it won't be my feast.'

'A feast is a feast,' mother says. 'Now it's time to go home. We have a lot of work to do tomorrow to get everything ready for our distinguished guests.'

'Come on,' Amrita says. 'The sooner we start, the sooner we finish.'

There are times when I could happily slap my sister.

'Do you think that they will put a girl forward to be a Chosen Woman?' I ask as we walk home.

'I believe that it has been agreed. It doesn't mean that the envoy will accept the offer no matter what father says,' Amrita replies. Her voice sounds brittle, like when you step on dry twigs. My sister is devout, hardworking and a brilliant weaver, but she is plain looking.

'Mayu or Rontu are just as likely to be selected as I am,' I say.

Amrita stops and looks at me. 'You don't believe that. You are the most beautiful girl in the valley, as Father is always telling anyone who will listen.'

'That doesn't mean that they agree with him.' I'm not to blame for father's boasting.

'Do you want to be a Chosen Woman?' Amrita asks which I think is a strange question.

'Yes, of course, I do,' I say, 'I would love to see Cusco and all its wonders.'

'You want fine clothes and to live in a palace.'

'Yes. I want all of that too. What's wrong with wanting a different life? You're just jealous,' I say.

'I'm not jealous. I believe that Inti should be our guide for how to live our lives.'

'So, what if Inti plans for me to marry the Inca and live in Cusco? You don't know what he wants for me or you.'

'You're right,' Amrita says. 'No one knows what Inti has planned for them. We can only pray and wait for his guidance and accept whatever he decrees.'

There's no point continuing to talk to Amrita, she's gone holy on me and will only lecture me about following the true path. Before I go to sleep, I ask Inti to bless my family and, if he wills, to let me be a Chosen Woman.

The Tavern
Sarah Aust

I met Derek in The Tavern the first time I ever went. I was cleaning the urinals of all things, holding my breath. You didn't need to go into the Gents to smell them, you sometimes caught a whiff when you were stood at the bar, but inside was a whole new layer of hell.

I'd just sprayed the urinals with bleach when Derek came in, already unzipping his flies. He scowled at me and looked over at the cubicle but there was someone already in there. He just used the urinal next to the one I was scrubbing. Derek never did stand on ceremony. I didn't know where to look so I grabbed my stuff and went to clean the Ladies.

The Ladies weren't much better. You were lucky if there was a seat on the loos, and someone had kicked a hole in the wall. They never fixed it in all the time I was going there. I won't tell you some of the things I saw in there, it's best left to the imagination.

Still, that was the first and last time I cleaned at The Tavern thanks to Derek. He insisted on buying me a drink once I'd finished, wouldn't take no for an answer even though I was meant to go onto The Swan and clean there. He insisted I had a small glass of wine even though I prefer bitter, pints of bitter that is. When I finished, he insisted I had another. I offered him my number, said I had to go to the The Swan but, like I said, you didn't say no to Derek.

Mrs Watts, I think her name was, from the agency let me go, just sent me a text telling me not to bother coming back. I wasn't that fussed about the job, but I was a bit worried about the money. More than that I was worried about spending all the extra time with Mom. I know she was my Mom, but she was bloody hard work and impossible to please. I couldn't tell her

I'd got the sack; I'd never hear the last of it.

I was at Derek's when I found the text from Mrs Watts. It was half-eight and I was trying to get back to sleep on his lumpy couch. I'd woken from a drunken slumber at around five in the morning and crawled there from his bed because he was lying on his back snoring loud enough to wake the dead. I got to know that couch quite well over the years. At about nine I gave up trying to sleep and was getting dressed, I really needed to go home and check on Mom. I really should have let her know where I was to be honest, she was old and would get confused about the slightest of things. If she didn't get confused, she'd get mad, just like she always had done.

Trouble was I couldn't get the door open. Derek had several locks and bolts on. It took me a while to find the keys and a bit longer to work out what key went where. And the bolts were bloody stiff. It took me a couple of goes to do the first one and I never got to the second.

'Where'd you think you're going?'

Derek was standing behind me wearing just his pants, his beer belly spilling over them.

'I need to check on Mom'

'Pah,' Derek said. 'Stick the kettle on, will you woman?'

'But me Mom', I said.

'She's a grown woman Bab, she'll be fine. Now stick the kettle on.'

Derek's eyes popped out of his head, so I did what I was told. I got to learn what the look meant; Derek always kept his keys on him after that.

The kitchen was filthy, I did sort that out, but he never would let me have a new one. He never let me have a new anything, so I put up with the cooker with the broken grill, the kitchen cupboards with the doors hanging off, the stained carpets and the lumpy sofa.

Mom ended up in a home. I did get to see her now and again when Derek wasn't around. Trouble was, he usually was. Sometimes she'd be pleased to see me even if she couldn't remember my name, she'd smile from ear to ear and hold my hand and didn't want to let go. Other times she'd glare and tell me to fuck off. It wasn't a bad thing as I never had long.

Derek never met my mom, didn't even go to the funeral. I went, I insisted on that. Derek didn't like it, but it was my mom. It was just me and Mrs Jones from next door, and a couple of the staff from the home. Mrs Jones didn't speak, just looked at me daggers and left.

After I hurried to The Tavern. Derek bought me a drink and Rita asked how it went. I said it went okay and they carried on talking about the Villa or whatever it was they were on about.

We always went to The Tavern. It was just a small place, one room with a raised area that had a pool table and a few tables and chairs. There was a platform where the DJ usually was and where the odd band played. The Tavern was dimly lit with small windows at the front. Some people would call it dingy and depressing. We went every bloody day.

Eventually Derek let me drink Carling like him, once he worked out that it was cheaper than wine. We always saw the same people in The Tavern; Rita the landlady with the spiky hair and the hard face, John and Sue, Jason and Kayleigh and all the men who came every day to escape their wives.

There was always music and it was always loud. The DJ usually started early; old hits blasting out and flashing lights. It would be like a Friday night inside, but you could step outside into bright sunshine and pop to the supermarket or wherever and it would be like any other Monday afternoon.

The fights started early too. Not every day though. Derek never started a fight, but he often got involved, separating people though, telling them to cut it out. People always did what Derek said.

The police came sometimes, often the same ones. They would threaten to take Rita's licence. She would roll her eyes and bar the troublemakers for a while and things would settle down. Everyone knew Derek and me in The Tavern. They would make a bee line for him and nod at me. We knew all about their lives, and they about ours although there wasn't much to tell. We were all always in The Tavern.

There were the odd changes there though, occasionally a barmaid left and there'd be someone new, but not often. The word barmaid never suited any of them though. They were always like Rita, hard faced like they were used to fighting. Most had short hair, tattoos and lined faces from all the fags. People rarely messed with them. Sometimes the regulars would die, like when Kayleigh's Jason got killed on his motorbike and when Gerry, the old Irishman who sat in one corner, just got thinner and thinner and one day he wasn't there anymore.

They'd have the wake at The Tavern. Rita would make sandwiches and get sausage rolls and things like that from Iceland. We would talk about the 'deceased' for a bit and Rita would stick the order of service from the funeral on the shelf above the bar. There was a sea of faces on that shelf, people that I'd known and plenty that I hadn't. Once you were above the bar people soon stopped talking about them, unless someone suddenly remembered something funny they'd said or done.

Derek's wife, Maureen, was one of the faces. The picture was an old one, when she was young and glamourous, before the cancer got her. Lung cancer. She was all dolled up with makeup and a red dress and her hair was a shiny dark brown. Derek didn't like me wearing make-up and it was too much hassle to insist. I always wondered if she somehow knew about me, if she was jealous.

Sometimes Derek's kids would come down, Emma and James. They would all talk about old times, about Maureen, about holidays and stuff like that. They never spoke to me. I would be stood there at the bar like a lemon. I might talk to Sue a bit or Rita, but they never said much. Sometimes I would pop out to the shops down the High Street, but Derek didn't like me doing that and it was better not to, to be honest. If Derek wanted some fags or something for his tea, I'd pop out but that was it.

I did make the most of it though, sometimes I'd pop to Greggs and get a Belgian bun and go and hide in the churchyard, round the back of the church and eat it. I'd have to be quick though, so Derek didn't wonder where I was. He used to call me fat, poke me in the belly, call it my beer belly. He had a cheek with the size of his. The funny thing was, I'd lost weight since I took up with him, didn't eat much and tried not to overdo the drinking, making each pint last. It helped me keep my wits about me.

I'd been with Derek about three years or so when things began to change. This new family moved into the estate. They were called Hunter. Rita said they'd been moved from Nechells because of trouble there. There were loads of them. They took up three flats, two on the same landing and one on the floor above. Not in our block thank God, but near enough so we could hear the parties and the rows. Between them and Derek snoring, I got next to no sleep.

One night we got back around eleven. There'd been nothing unusual that day. We got to The Tavern just after lunchtime and stopped until closing. Derek was pissed off because James was supposed to come down, but he never showed up. I was just glad to be going home. I'd got quite pissed because I really wanted to sleep; I was bloody knackered anyway.

We could hear it before we even turned into our street. It was a massive party. There were cars parked everywhere on our street, double parked and even on the pavement. It looked like the party was spread out over at least two of the flats. I wondered what went on at those parties. I'd probably hate it, but you never know.

'Fuck's sake,' said Derek. 'Bloody noisy twats, think they own the whole street.'

'Don't worry, Derek,' I said, 'you'll sleep through it, you always do.'

He glared at me and my heart skipped a beat. 'Not the point,' he said, jabbing me painfully in the chest. 'Think about the old people around here'

I didn't answer. Derek never seemed worried about my lack of sleep, and it didn't seem like a good idea to mention it. Once we got in, it sounded like the party was happening in our flat, but I wasn't that bothered because I was about to pass out. Derek stomped about like a bear with a sore head then pulled back the lounge curtains and glared out towards the Hunter's. It was like he thought they'd take notice of that.

'Derek, just come to bed, will you?'

He turned around and said, 'Don't tell me what to do, woman.'

I just went into the bedroom and lay down. I thought Derek would follow, but I just zonked out. When I woke up again it was about half three and my tongue was stuck to the top of my mouth. I could still hear the party, but I couldn't hear Derek. Even the odd time when he slept on the sofa, I could still hear the snores.

I wanted a glass of water, so I got out of bed and carefully opened the bedroom door. Derek wasn't there which was very odd. I got my water and downed it. Then I needed the loo. When I came back there was still no sign of Derek. Maybe I should've looked for him then, but I was still knackered, and it was good to have the bed to myself.

Next time I woke it was half six. My mouth was dry again but the first thing I noticed was the quiet. It was deathly. The party was over, and Derek was still not in bed and I could hear nothing from the lounge. All I could hear was my own breathing and the odd cheep from the birds outside.

I checked the lounge but still no Derek. My heart started to beat a bit fast and then I noticed the flat door was open slightly.

Derek was still really careful about the door; he still locked and double bolted the door and kept the keys on him. His baseball bat was missing too. That's when I knew something was up. I put my shoes and coat on and left the flat. It was starting to get light, but it was still quite dim out there.

I went down the stairs and I was just turning onto the last flight when I saw Derek. He was slumped on the stairs near the bottom, the baseball bat had rolled away from him and was lying against the door to the block. His mouth was open, but he wasn't snoring, and his eyes were open too. His face was grey when normally it was red.

I knew he was dead before I touched him, but I still had to check. He was cold. He didn't go peacefully that's for sure, his eyes weren't just open, they were bulging the way they always did when he was on one and he was snarling like a starving guard dog. I pulled my tongue out at him then walked slowly back upstairs to get my phone.

We went back to The Tavern after the funeral. It was the usual affair. Rita had laid on a few plates of sandwiches, some vol-au-vents and some of those Chinese party snacks. Rita popped Derek's order of service above the bar and everyone raised a glass. James and Emma didn't talk to me.

I kept going back for a while, but no-one talked to me much. They had put Derek next to Sandra so they both looked down on me from there. By the second week after the funeral they hardly mentioned him anymore. On the Wednesday I was bored by the end of my first pint. I fancied a Belgian bun, so I went and got one. I didn't make an excuse before I went, never said 'bye'. I just went.

Once the bun was in my hands, I wasn't sure what to do. There was no need to hide nor to rush back. I sat on a bench by the churchyard wall in full view of the High Street and took my time. People walked past as I ate, they may or may not have noticed me. When it was gone, I looked back towards The Tavern. I brushed the crumbs from my lap and got up and walked off in the direction of The Matthew Murdock.

The Murdock was just a chain pub looked down upon by many. I'd not been since before Derek. It was modern and light and served proper beer. I ordered a pint and started to plan. I never went back to The Tavern.

Murder at the Eagle
S.W. Mackman

Mary screams. Blood is dripping into a small pool on the carpet under Brian's chair. She runs across the room, knocking several glasses and grabs his shoulder.

'Brian. Say something!'

Brian doesn't say anything. Instead, he slumps forwards revealing a chair sodden in blood and a needle-like knife pointing through the back from behind. Mary collapses to the floor. Why the extreme reaction? I mean, I'm shocked, but I'm not crying.

Clare is on my right on one of the comfy chairs. She's Brian's wife. Tears are slowly forming on her face. It must be terrible to see your husband die. They'd been married almost thirty years. She glances at Richard and he puts his hand on her knee.

'Can we have some quiet please, Jenny is reading,' said Linda, her sharp voice cutting through Mary's weeping.

I glance around the room. There are about a dozen of us sitting in a haphazard circle. Everyone is focused on Mary who is now stroking Brian's grey straggly hair. Jenny was reading from her novel but she's put down her laptop. She doesn't look like she's going to continue. Dave was down to his boxers when she stopped. Her description of his legs almost gave me palpitations. I really wanted to hear what happened next.

The Eagle writer's club has never seen anything like this. The biggest scandal up to now was when Brian's stamp collection went missing. Talk of that lasted weeks.

'Quiet,' says Linda. No one takes any notice. 'Under section 6.4 clause 5 I'm suspending this meeting.'

"What's she doing on the floor crying? He's my husband. I knew there was something going on. I could see it,' says Clare.

"It must be terrible for you,' says Richard. His hand is still on her knee. I wouldn't let him touch me like that.

We hang around waiting for the police. No one stops me taking photos of the knife although I do get some dirty looks. Soon an ambulance arrives. Not much for them to do except take the body away. Then the police. They keep us all in and start asking questions.

How could anyone have stabbed him? It must have been someone in the room.

'What's your name?' a nice-looking policeman says to me.

'Sally Smith,' I say. His name is Michael and he asks me what happened.

I tell him that Brian didn't say much all evening. He was definitely alive when he walked in. It was his turn to read first but he said he wanted to use the time to discuss a serious matter. Maybe someone wanted to silence him. Linda didn't let him talk though. She was a stickler for the rules and quoted the constitution,

'Under section 4.3 clause 2 if a slot becomes vacant, work by new members get preference. This club needs change. Writing is important but we need to embrace contemporary art forms and encourage younger members. Older members don't own this club and can't just do what they like.'

She let a twenty-something who I'd never seen before perform a piece called The Blazing Forest using the medium of mime.

When that was over we had a break and everyone went to the bar to get a drink. Everyone except Brian. I really needed a gin and tonic. He sat in his chair by the door looking serious. He didn't talk to anyone. I distinctly remember that because I noticed his Union Flag badge on his lapel as I walked out. There's not many Brexit supporters around here. It makes me so sad that 2020 will be remembered as the year of Brexit. There's not much he can do to stop her now. There's an EGM

135

next month with an agenda pushing alternate art forms.
I was last in the queue for the bar and I bought me and Julie a drink. We all had to walk past Brian's chair. I suppose anyone could have secretly stuck a knife through the back as we walked past. Anyone who hadn't got two handfuls of drink. It's amazing how he said nothing. Maybe he groaned a little, but that's what he did normally. He was always grumbling about things whether it was politics, the weather or his bones. The knife did look very thin and very sharp. Maybe he didn't notice. Maybe it just felt like background noise amidst all his other pains. He just sat there bleeding to death without realising. He'd have certainly made a fuss if he could.
It wasn't until ten minutes into Jenny's reading that Mary screamed.

    'So, who did it?' I say.

    'I couldn't possibly say,' says Michael.

    'I bet you've got an idea. It's usually the wife isn't it. Especially when he's having an affair. Do you think she did it? What about Linda?'

Michael gives me a look. But he still gives me his number and asks me to contact him if I think of anything else.

When I get home, I notice the coin in my purse. A brand new shiny 50p. 'Peace prosperity and friendship with all nations 31 January 2020,' is proudly written on the back. It's the new Brexit coin. I paid for the drink with cash. It must have been given to me in my change.
I hardly sleep that night. The events of the previous day are going around and around my mind. I get up at 2am to research knives. Who made it? Where could you buy it from? If I'm going to uncover what happened I'll need to visit Brian and Clare's house.

I've got their address although I've never been inside. I leave it a couple of days and then knock on her door in the afternoon. She looks pleased to see me.

    'I'm so sorry about what happened. It must be so awful. How are you doing?' I say.

    'Lovely to see you Sally. Not very well to be honest. It's all so hard to take in.'

She invites me to sit in her living room.

'What have you done these past two days,' I say.

'I've been shopping. But I haven't been to work. I've stayed mostly in the house,' says Clare. I lean back in my chair. It's comfortable although it's strange talking to someone sitting below a picture of Margaret Thatcher.

'I think it's good for you to get out,' I say. I can't think of anything more useful.

'They are going to do a post-mortem. I can't organise a funeral. I can't get a death certificate. I can't see his body. I feel so helpless.'

'You need to look after yourself.' I pause for a bit and then notice something. 'Are these his short stories?' I point to a CD on a coffee table with beautifully carved legs. It is helpfully labelled Short Stories. He'd written several bestselling novels. He seemed to be able to come up with ideas on demand. It probably contained stories I'd never heard. Who knows how many there were.

'Yes. He put it there a few days ago. I didn't take much notice. Would you like some tea?'

'Oh, that would be lovely. Are you sure you don't want me to make it?' I didn't come in to be waited on.

'No, love. That's fine. It's lovely to have a visitor. I haven't had many people round. Richard's a good friend and he's been checking on me, but otherwise not many. He enjoys coming round and he gets lonely in his flat.'

'Do you mind if I use your bathroom?'

I go up the stairs. The first door on the left has a large union flag stuck to it and also some unusual stickers. It takes me a few moments to realise some are logos of knife manufacturers I noticed on the internet. I stand outside and listen. Nothing. I push the door gently. It opens. It must be her son Dan's bedroom. I thought teenagers were supposed to have pictures of singers on their wall not angry middle-aged men. The wooden surface of the desk has been damaged by something sharp especially near the laptop. Curiosity takes hold of me and I open the top draw. It's crammed with coke cans, crisp packets, and a bottle of cider. I feel quite relieved at seeing something I can relate to. The next one contains a collection of knives. They aren't cooking knives. They look very dangerous.

I've seen enough. I wipe over where I've touched with my jumper to get rid of my fingerprints. Better find the bathroom quick.

The tea is given to me in a china cup poured from a proper tea pot. Very nice. Clare sits down in the chair opposite.

'Why did she have to do it? It's so selfish of her.' Clare's looking at me intensely.

'Who are you talking about?'

'Linda of course. All we wanted was a nice little group where we could read our stories. But she had to change it all. Rules. Constitution. Nonsense. She must have hated him so much. But to murder him as well. Why?'

'Are you sure it was her?'

'Who else could it be? Wasn't it enough to take control of the club?' I glance around the room. The bookshelves look packed. Mostly novels but I also see something about the Stuarts. Two shelves of Wisden does seem a little excessive.

'Did you find the bathroom OK?' she asks.

'Yes, fine', I reply.

'You didn't go into any of the other rooms by accident?'

'No. Why do you ask?'

'Oh. No reason.'

'You've got two milk jugs,' I say as she's pouring my milk.
She then pours milk from the other into her tea.

'Yes. But none of them match the cups. I couldn't see the proper one. Things are just going missing. Why can't I find them?'

'But why two?'

'Oh, mine is almond milk. I don't like cow's milk.'

'I didn't know you are lactose intolerant.'

I pick up the cup. It has an exquisite flower pattern. I put it close to my mouth and feel the steam on my face. The smell is slightly unusual. I ask her about Mary.

"The harlot. But it was me he loved. She was just a fling,' says Clare. 'He'd just started using aftershave. I knew something was up. I never confronted him with it. But it's happened before and nothing came of it then. He was still with

138

me on the day he died. I thought she was my friend. How could she?'

I turn the conversation to something less controversial. The room is looking very good. She said that she hates the colour but Brian had insisted.

'Drink your tea up, there's more in the pot,' she adds.
I say her daffodils are lovely. Brian had planted them. She wanted a fuchsia bush there but he wouldn't let her. Then she starts complaining about the council rubbish collection.

I've had enough. I make an excuse about being late for a dental appointment and leave. It's not like me not to touch my tea but that house made me feel uneasy.

On Sunday I see Clare and Richard in a cafe together on the high street sitting next to the large window and I take my chance.

'Hi,' I say. 'Lovely to see you all.'

'Hello,' says Clare. I pull up a chair and join them without being asked. They are sharing a large slice of cake. I give them a bit of small talk then slip in,

'How are you going to manage now he's gone?'

'I should be OK,' Clare says. That was quite revealing.

'Did you know that Richard has had a short story anthology accepted for publication by Penguin books? Isn't that great,' says Clare. The cake is calling me. It looks so moist. I reach behind and grab a fork.

'No, I didn't. That's really good. Well done,' I manage to say. I am more than a little surprised. The last short story he wrote he called Pirates of the Coventry Canal, and with its emphasis on shipping timetables, it just didn't do it for me.

I change the subject.

'What about all Brian's stuff. He did like collecting things didn't he,' I say and take a forkful of cake.

'I haven't thought about it,' says Clare.

'I heard he collected coins. Is that true?' I say swallowing quickly.

'Yes, he did,' says Clare.

'Did he get hold of one of the Brexit coins?'

'Yes. How did you know that? He was very proud of it. In twenty years they're going to be worth a lot.'

'Now he's gone would you sell it?' I say.

'Why are you so interested in Brexit coins? I've really not thought about it. My husband has just died. I don't care about Brexit coins,' says Clare. I need to calm her down, but I can't. My mouth is stuffed with cake.

'I'm sorry. I shouldn't have asked. That was too personal,' I finally get out.

'Yes,' says Richard.

'The cake's really good,' I say.

'I wouldn't know, you've eaten most of it,' says Richard. They don't want to talk to me, but I've got what I need.

'Nice to meet you. I've got to rush though. Clare, when you get home check that Brexit coin of yours. Is it still there?' I say. I pull out my chair and leave.

It's going round and round my head. Mary, Richard, Clare. All the people I've spoken to. Then I realise what happened. There is only one explanation that fits all the facts. I text Michael, the hot-looking policeman. I tell him about the knife collection and that I think one of his knives was the murder weapon. I tell him that something is going to happen at the next club meeting. He needs to be there.

He replies almost immediately. He says that Dan isn't in the club and can't be a suspect.

I know that I text him. Someone took the knife and then used it.

On Tuesday when we all gather at the back room of the Eagle there isn't the usual chatter. Still there's a bigger crowd than usual. Maybe they've just come to be part of the drama. I arrived early to bag one of the comfy chairs, and found a safe spot for my wine. Michael arrives later. He stands at the back by the door just where Brian was killed. He's looking very good in his body armour.

Linda does the opening and we all introduce ourselves. Before she has a chance to hand over to the opening speaker I say in my best assertive voice,

'I have an emergency point to make.'

'So, what section of the constitution allows you to do this?' says Linda. 'The opening speaker is Dave.'

'Someone was murdered here. I know who did it. There's a policeman here waiting to hear what I say,' I say. I glance at Michael. He nods.

'What do you know? I need to know who killed him,' says Mary.

Linda doesn't say anything. She slumps back and looks at the floor.

'Thank you. Let's go through the suspects. First Linda.' I'm looking at her as I say this and she starts to glare at me through narrow eyes.

'She's changing the club. Brian hated it. He wanted somewhere informal where he could read his stories. Linda wants something different. They really didn't like each other. But she didn't kill him. Why should she? She's the one with the power here. So, let's move on. Clare, did you check your Brexit coin?'

'The coin? It's gone missing.'

'Yes, I thought so. Back to Clare. Brian betrayed her. Mary was in love with him. They were having an affair. Probably been sending her texts for months. Did you notice how he started liking Mary's Facebook posts? He was successful even if he was a bit crabby and Mary fell for him. I believe the knife that killed him belonged to their son. Dan has a very unhealthy interest in knives by the way. By killing him she could rid herself of him and get herself a new boyfriend. The royalties from Brian's books won't stop just because he's dead and maybe there's some life insurance? Some widows are hard up. Not her.'

'That's a horrible thing to say. I didn't do it! I thought you were being my friend when you came round.'

'You didn't do it. Most of the facts point to you. But not all. The one issue that it kept on coming back to me was the change I got at the bar. They gave me a Brexit coin. A shiny 50p celebrating Brexit.

I googled it. They are uncirculated. You can buy them for ten pounds from the royal mint. Now I think that's a rip off. That's over two gin and tonics and I know which I'd choose. Why would anyone who is willing to buy one of those for ten pounds then use it so soon after Brexit? I remember my Mum showing me her Charles and Diana coin she was given when she was

young. It was only worth 25p but she'd kept it all these years and it was still in its original plastic case.
Someone spent it and it ended up in my purse as change. The only people who supported Brexit around here were Brian and possibly Clare. He didn't buy any drinks. She did.
Imagine you've just killed your husband. Would your first act be to spend his Brexit money? That wouldn't be on your mind and you'd have no reason to use it. It would be like spending your own keepsake. But what if you stole the money and had just killed him? Buying drinks with it would be an act of victory. But who stole the money?
It was Richard. You befriended Clare. You made frequent visits to their house.'

'I've had enough of this nonsense. I'm leaving,' says Richard standing up and marching to the door.

'Stay where you are,' says Michael. He moves a step to his left blocking the exit.

'But you stole more than just the Brexit coin. I bet you got quite a few things from Brian and Clare's house. The main thing you stole though was a collection of Brian's stories. Then you sent them to a publisher under your own name. Maybe you edited them a little to change a few details. You must have been in a terrible rush to kill him, once the book was out. That's really very bad organisation. When the police search your flat, I think they will find a nice little collection of Brian's belongings. Maybe a copy of the original stories.'

'I hated him,' shouted Richard. 'I spent years trying to get to know Mary. Then one day he decides he likes her and she just comes running. It was like I wasn't there.'

Panacea
T.B. Donne

Mary poured herself a large brandy and downed it in a few gulps. She lay down on the sofa and let the sound of the TV lull her to sleep. She woke at midnight and stumbled up to bed, opened the bedroom window wide, lay down and pulled the thin fleece over her.

A wave of heat engulfed her and she felt like she was suffocating. She threw back the fleece and there was a moment of relief and then the cold bit into her. She covered herself and felt a slick of sweat form between her arms and her body.

Even though she was roasting she made herself keep the cover in place. She fought off panic by counting her breaths. It was getting light by the time she fell asleep.

She slept through her alarm and got to work late. Her colleagues sat at their computers in jumpers and cardigans,

while she sat in a thin, sleeveless top, sweat prickling her scalp.
Her boss asked her to finish off the Luxmore account and have the file printed out and on her desk by the end of the day. That was so typical, leaving things to the last minute and then expecting her to sort out the mess, on top of her other workload.
She worked all morning on the account, and by lunchtime her eyes were burning. She tried to print it out but there was a paper jam. She pulled out the paper tray, lifted the flaps front and back and peered inside but she couldn't see anything jammed.

'Do you want me to have a look?' asked Lucy, who was young and helpful and had a way with technology.

'It's ridiculous. How am I supposed to get anything done?'

Mary slammed the paper drawer back into the machine. 'I'm going out for a sandwich and some fresh air.'

'Could you get me some hula-hoops?' Lucy asked.
'No I can't,' Mary said. She left the office, banging the door behind her.

A man was sitting on the ground outside Sainsburys. He had dirty hands, brown teeth and a gormless grin.

'Spare some change please?'

Mary ignored him. 'Useless waste of a human life,' she thought.

'How's he going to change anything, sitting on the ground all day? He must get benefits. He's obviously getting enough to eat. If people stop giving him money, he'd soon give up and then we wouldn't have him sitting there, making us feel guilty for having jobs and homes.'

At the crossroads there was a triangle of grass with benches and a cherry tree. It would have been a lovely place to eat lunch but the benches were always occupied by grubby, red-faced street drinkers.

Mary ate her sandwich at her desk. She saw Lucy cringe in mock terror and heard Sandra giggle. No doubt they had been talking about her. She ignored them. Her desk was covered in papers. How was she supposed to think amid all this mess? She gathered them all up and fed them into the shredder.

She switched on her computer, stared blankly at the screen and emptied her recycle bin while she tried to remember what she was doing. She hadn't got a clue and went to make a coffee to clear her head.

'I sorted the printer,' Lucy said. 'I put your stuff on your desk.'

Mary felt sick and rushed back to her computer. She searched everywhere for the Luxmore file but it had disappeared. She put her head in her hands and cried.

Her boss told her to go home and sort herself out. Lucy looked at her with concern and touched her shoulder but Mary shrugged her off and told her to leave her alone.

Mary went to her GP surgery to make an appointment.

'The next available appointment is in three weeks.'
'I am not waiting that long!'
'Please, don't shout.'
'I'm not shouting.'
'Please don't cry.......oh. Is it....' the receptionist leaned forward and mouthed the words 'the change?'

Mary nodded.

The receptionist smiled. 'There is a special evening clinic with Dr Sri.' She opened a little red diary on her desk.

'Can you do this evening? Eight o'clock?'

Mary nodded. The receptionist wrote in the diary.

'See you at eight. The door will be closed. Just ring the bell. You'll like Dr Sri. She's lovely.'

When Mary went back the surgery was in darkness. She rang the bell and the lights went on inside. The door was unlocked by a stately woman wearing a lilac dress and jacket.

'Mary?' she extended her hand.

'Yes.' Mary shook her hand and Dr Sri's gold bangles jingled. She led the way through to her consulting room.

'Sit down and tell me all about it.'

She listened without interruption while Mary told her all about her misery.

'I know it's just the menopause but I can't cope. I think I need to go onto HRT.'

'You could, or you could try this,' Dr Sri said, opening her desk drawer and taking out a small, white box.

Written on it in swirly gold writing was the word Panacea.

'This is something new, quite marvellous really. Take

one tonight before you go to sleep. Just let it dissolve on your tongue.'

'Just one tablet?'

'Oh yes. The effects are very long lasting. When the benefits start to wear off, come back and see me.'

Mary opened the white box. Inside on a white satin insert was a golden pill. She put it in on her tongue and let it dissolve; it tasted like honey. She lay down and fell fast asleep.

She woke up early. Her head was clear and she didn't have a single ache or pain. She sang as she showered. She looked in the mirror to put on her makeup and realised there was no need. Her skin was smooth, her eyes were bright and her hair was perfect.

Work was a breeze. Lucy told her to look in her recent files folder and there was the Luxmore account, safe and sound. Mary took lunchtime orders from everybody and strolled to Sainsburys.

The man outside the supermarket looked sad.

'What kind of life is that?' Mary thought, 'sitting on the ground all day, hoping for a bit of change. His poor legs and back must ache.'

She got cash from the cashpoint to buy her shopping so that she could give him some change. The supermarket was delightful, with all its beautiful fruit and bright, exciting packaging. The music made her want to dance down the aisles.

On her way out, she gave him five pounds. 'Thanks, you're an angel,' he said, beaming. 'You're very welcome,' she said, beaming back.

Next lunchtime, the man stood up.

'I don't like to ask but I wondered if you could help me.'

'Of course. What is it?'

'It's my Mum's funeral this afternoon. It's in Manchester, only I haven't got enough money for the train there.'

'How much do you need?'

'It's thirty pounds, but I don't expect you to give me all of it.'

Mary didn't hesitate. She took thirty pounds out of the cashpoint and gave it to him. 'Thank you, I'll pay you back.'

'There's no need. Take care, I'm sorry about your Mum.'

On her way home from work, Mary saw him staggering down the pavement with a can in his hand. She felt stupid for believing his stories.

In time, the good effects of the Panacea wore off and she went back to see Dr Sri and get some more. On the doctor's desk was a turquoise metal box.

'I am glad it worked so well. Unfortunately, there is a price to pay if you want some more.'

'I don't mind. How much are they?' Mary asked, opening her handbag.

'You can't buy them with money.' Dr Sri tapped the side of the box. 'This device takes life force and uses it to generate Panacea.' She opened the box and took out a pair of pink gloves wrapped in cellophane.

'You collect life force using these.' She waved the gloves. 'They are impregnated with a painless, untraceable poison. They dispatch the life force donor and harvest their life credits.'

'So, to get more Panacea, I have to kill people?' Mary put her hands on her knees and closed her eyes.

When she opened them, Dr Sri offered her a glass of water. It was cold and tasted sweet.

'I popped in a Panacea to help with the shock,' Dr Sri said.

'Thank you.' Mary sipped the water and soon felt calm. 'I don't think I can kill anyone.'

'I'm not forcing you to do anything you don't want to,' Dr Sri said. 'Take the gloves and think about it, the instructions are on the back. If you find it's not for you, you can always go onto HRT.'

In spite of the Panacea, Mary still felt rather disconcerted by Dr Sri's suggestion. She went to Sainsburys to buy something comforting for supper.

He was sitting outside Sainsburys as always, the scrounging liar. When he saw her, he stood up. He looked solemn.

'Can you help me please angel? It's my Mum's funeral tomorrow but it's in Nottingham and I need £30 to get there.'

'I thought she died last month,' Mary said. His face

hardened.

'Do I look like a walking piggy bank?' Mary said.

His face reddened.

'F**k off you c**t.' His breath stank.

She recoiled, wiping her face and sought refuge in the supermarket.

She bought chicken soup, carrot cake and a bottle of brandy to calm her nerves. She walked slowly round the aisles feeling reluctant to go outside and face more abuse. How dare she sit there, making it an ordeal to go to her own supermarket. To her relief, when she left, he had gone.

After supper she read the glove's instructions. They said the gloves were harmless until activated and this was done by clasping the donor's hand firmly for five seconds at which point they would vibrate. Once used they should be removed carefully, turning them inside out and kept in their packaging until they could be measured.

Next time she went to Sainsburys she tested the waters by giving him a pound which he took with his usual stupid smile. He showed no signs of recognition or resentment.

It was only when the hot flushes returned, accompanied by insomnia, confusion, forgetfulness and extreme irritation that she decided to kill him. He was in his usual spot, lowering the tone of the place. She stood next to him and shivered.

'Gosh, it's getting nippy,' she said, taking the pink gloves out of her bag, unwrapping them and pulling them on.

'It was freezing last night,' he said, shuddering and wiping his nose on his hand.

'Isn't it funny. I've seen you around for ages and I don't even know your name.

She leaned down and held out her hand. 'I'm Mary.'

'I'm Stuart.' he said, extending his.

'Pleased to meet you Stuart.'

She gripped his hand and counted to five and the gloves vibrated.

'Ow! Static,' he said, snatching his hand away and rubbing it.

'So sorry,' she said, peeling off her gloves and putting them safely away.

It was best to be polite in case they didn't work. His head

dropped forward onto his chest and his arms dangled by his sides. He looked like another drunken beggar.

When Mary saw the scrappy and pathetic bunches of flowers left on the pavement where he used to sit, she felt sad but also glad to know she had succeeded and would soon be able to get her medicine. She rang the surgery and three evenings later was in Dr Sri's consulting room.

'Are you sure he didn't suffer?' Mary asked.

'I'm positive, now where are the gloves?'

Dr Sri put them in the metal box and after a short while the box chimed. She opened a little drawer at the bottom and tipped out twelve golden tablets. She put eleven into a small jar and hesitated.

'You look like you could do with one now.'

Mary ate the twelfth tablet and relief spread through her.

'Here are a couple of pairs of gloves. I'll see you in about a year.'

The Village Green looked beautiful. One of the benches was free and Mary sat down, closed her eyes and turned her face to the sun.

'Spare some change please?'

She squinted at a middle-aged man bundled up in many layers despite the heat. 'I don't think I've got any change,' she said, feeling disappointed.

'Sorry to have bothered you. Have a nice day.' He turned to walk away.

'Would you like a sweet?' Mary said.

'I don't really like them.'

'These are good for you. They're like vitamins,'

Mary said, showing him the jar. The Panacea glowed in the sun.

'Go on then' he said, holding out his hand.

Mary tipped one into his palm then noticed how pale and thin he was and tipped out another.

'Ta love.'

He put them into his mouth and sighed with pleasure.

He unshouldered his heavy pack and sat down with it at his feet.

'I used to work there,' he said, pointing to the cafe across the road.

'What happened?'

'I had a car accident and couldn't work. My housing benefits got screwed up and I lost my flat. I've been on the streets ever since.'

'How long for?'

'Seven years.'

'I'm so sorry.'

'Thanks for listening and thanks for the sweet. You sure it wasn't an E? I feel lovely.' He shouldered his backpack. 'See you later, yeah?'

Mary looked after him and wiped her eyes. People were really nice, she thought.

On the other bench, a red-faced man and a woman with long white hair were sharing a bottle of Frosty Jack.

She went over to them.

'Would you like a sweet?'

'Ta love,' the woman said, holding out her hand.

Mary tipped three Panacea into her palm.

'I don't want any of that s**t,' the man roared, dashing the jar out of Mary's grip. It smashed on the ground and the pills scattered everywhere.

'S**t, s**t, s**t,' the man bellowed, stamping on the tablets and the glass. The woman shrieked with laughter.

'You are dead,' Mary said.

She kept the gloves in her handbag at all times, ready for any opportunity. At last she saw the red-faced man sitting on the Village Green on his own.

'Lovely weather we're having,' she said, sitting beside him and putting on the gloves.

He stared at her, befuddled. She took a five pound note out of her pocket and offered it to him. He took it and she closed both her hands round his but before she could count to five, she was thumped in the back.

'Get your f*****g hands off my man!' It was the white-haired woman. Mary stood up and backed away but the woman advanced, shoving her in the chest. She fell backwards and hit her head on the paving stones...

... 'Are you alright?' A young community police officer was leaning over her.

'Come on, let's get you off the floor.'

She clutched his bare arm as he helped her to a bench. She felt the glove vibrate. He sat her down and crouched in front of her, looking up into her face.

'How are you? Did you bang your heggh....'

He blinked, his eyes widened and he toppled over onto his side. An ambulance came with lights flashing and siren wailing but it left with both switched off. Guilt would not let her sleep. She was tormented by her memories of the young policeman's last moments. She could not bear it. She turned the last pair of poisoned gloves inside out, pulled them on, squeezed her hands together and counted to five. Cramp started in her fingers and spread like wildfire, from muscle to muscle until each one was a knot of agony.

At last, the cramp let go. Her mouth was full of blood where she had bitten her tongue. She had peed and pooed herself and the room stank of it. She undressed, slowly and shakily. She tried to take off the gloves but they seemed stuck to her hands. Her whole body was covered with dark bruises apart from her gloved hands which were still a jaunty pink. She put on her dressing gown and eased herself down the stairs on her bottom, step by step. She unscrewed the brandy bottle and drank from it. She tried to cry but it hurt her chest too much. She drank until her head spun and curled up on the sofa and slept with the bottle clutched to her chest.

She was woken by the doorbell which she ignored. There was a banging on the door and then shouting through the letterbox.

'Mary, it's Dr Sri. Let me in please. You need help.'

Mary wobbled her way to the front door and opened it.

It was Dr Sri. She looked excited and seemed to be emitting a ringing sound. She put her arm round Mary's waist and helped her back to the sofa. She reached into her shoulder bag, took out the turquoise metal box and put it on the coffee table. The ringing noise was coming from the box.

'I need Panacea,' Mary said.

'First, we need to get those gloves off you.' She went into the kitchen and Mary heard the tap running.

She returned carrying the washing up bowl, half filled with warm water. She took Mary's hands in hers and held them under the water.

The gloves became loose and Dr Sri tore them off and wrung

them out. She opened the box, dropped the gloves inside and closed the lid. The ringing stopped. She threw herself back on the sofa with a sigh.

'Now we wait.' she said.

'Please. Have you got any Panacea?' Mary said.

'Drink your brandy,' Dr Sri said, her eyes never leaving the box.

Mary took a slug of brandy. 'Did you know that it hurt? Being killed by those gloves?'

'You're not dead are you?'

'Yes but....'

'The Panacea slugged it out with the poison and kept you alive. That's why you're all black and blue.'

'It still might hurt to die from it.'

'Well nobody has survived so we can ask them, have they? Come on, come on....' She leaned forward, hands clenched, staring at the box.

The box started to chime rapidly. She reached out and opened the lid with a kind of reverence. It was full to the brim with Panacea. She tipped them onto the table and closed the lid again. Mary grabbed a handful and stuffed them in her mouth. The relief was incredible. The box chimed again.

Dr Sri opened it and it was full once more.

'What's happening?' Mary asked.

'Your gloves put the box into an infinity loop. From now on it will keep producing Panacea without any need for life credits.'

'Did you know this would happen?'

'Oh yes. I was just waiting to see which of my collectors would crack first.'

'What are you going to do with all that Panacea? Sell it?'

'No, I'm going to sell the box. I've already got a buyer lined up. I should get five million pounds for it. Thank you, Mary. You can keep those.'

She waved her hand at the gleaming pile on the table.

The Village Green was covered with snow and there were Christmas lights wound into the branches of the Cherry Tree. Mary had nearly recovered from the poisoning but she still felt fragile and easily moved by beautiful things. She stood gazing at the lights until she began to shiver.

The cafe looked inviting. Pushing open the door she noticed a sign which read 'Free hot drink and cake if you are homeless.' She swallowed and her eyes prickled.

She ordered a gingerbread latte and when the barista brought it over, he sat down opposite her.

'You don't remember me, do you?' he said.

She racked her brains but couldn't place him.

'You gave me two little gold sweets and they changed my life. I couldn't sleep that night. I got a four pack and cracked the first tin but I just didn't want it. I just kept looking up and the stars and the sky was so clear and black and it felt like my mind was getting huge and clearer.'

'The next day I walked into town; I was just so full of energy. I went to the Council Offices and walked in and said I needed somewhere to live and it was like they couldn't do enough for me. They gave me some emergency money and restarted my benefits and that night I was in my own room in a hostel. The day after that, I was still buzzing and itching to do something and ended up working in the kitchen there. I was in my element.'

'I missed the village though so I came back and they were advertising here for staff. Half an hour later, I'd got a job. Thank you.'

The door opened, bringing in a gust of chill air.

'Hello Annie, hello Seamus,' the barista said. Mary turned round. It was the white-haired woman and red-faced man who drank on The Green.

'Hello Jamie,' they said. They sat down at a table and he made them a pot of tea and delivered it along with two enormous wedges of chocolate cake. He sat back down at Mary's table.

'How can you afford to give free drinks and cakes?'

'People like giving a bit extra when they treat themselves.'

'Do Annie and Seamus often come in?'

'Every day.'

'Good. See you tomorrow.'

The cherry tree was in full blossom. Annie was planting primulas in the big wooden planters. Her white hair was pinned up and shone in the sunlight. Seamus was varnishing a bench. His face was ruddy with good health. A thin lad with his hood up despite the heat was picking up dog-ends off the floor and putting them in his pocket.

Mary came out of the cafe with two icy lemonades for the workers. She asked the lad if he would like a cold drink and he said he'd rather have a beer.

Jamie took a bottle of Sol out of the glass fronted fridge and levered off the cap. Mary dropped two Panacea into the bottle. She wiped her forehead with her sleeve.

'You look tired. Sit in the shade for a bit. I'll take it.' Jamie said.

Mary sat, feeling her heart thudding and heat enfolding her like an unwanted blanket. One little golden pill would make her better; but it wouldn't bring back the policeman she had killed and she chose not to take it in memory of him.

She looked out at Jamie, talking to the lad in the hoodie; unaware of how much his life was about to change.

Tumble Turn
Chris Randall

The abiding scent of Alex's childhood would always be the smell of chlorine. What had begun for him as a place of play, the pool had become the domain of hard competition. His existence had become defined by desperate thrashes of energy through the water, culminating in his palm thrust against tile. When he finished every sprint, he visualised himself crashing through the wall of the pool, the building itself and, in a spray of bricks, dust and water - cracking the world in half.

Alex was eleven when it first changed. He'd landed at Bishop Tranter and managed to stay put long enough for Mr Grigg, the PE teacher, to offer him a place on the school swimming squad. It turned out he had a natural talent for butterfly. For a stroke which many found difficult; the crucifying lunging of the upper body to clear each breath, he found he could easily dial this up or down according to the needs of each race. After all there was nothing so strenuous in the pool compared to the bullying of reality. When he started winning pieces of metal for his efforts, he realised he might be on to something.

Amanda, his foster mother at the time, was the one who started stitching his medals to a piece of blue cloth that she hung in his room. With one or two hanging in one corner, he had thought the gesture pointless. But when a quarter of it was covered with gleaming gold discs, he had a metric of worth. As he approached twelve it was so laden with polished brass that he knew for the first time in his life that he was doing something well. He was becoming a young sportsman. Then Marie, that jealous bitch whose pink bedroom he had borrowed, stole the banner and threatened to burn it. He had punched her hard in the face and been summarily returned to the care of the state for several weeks of therapy before the funding ran out. He wasn't allowed to go back to Amanda's house.

His temper was often the cause or effect of any trouble he found himself in. But, could he swim. There was just the need for water. To be on it, in it, or underneath it. Everything else fell away. There was no more noise. No distractions. No chats, or online cunts and their comments to contend with. It was the sedative which the social workers prescribed for any of his would-be foster parents. 'Alex is fine as long as you let him swim. As long as he can do that, you'll find he behaves.'

There were no takers. For a while he was stuck at Stanley House, for four months, then six, then twelve. There was a minder there, an ex-bodyguard called Vinnie with a bent face, more tamed animal than human. Vinnie gave him books and fitness magazines to read, and made the biggest change to Alex's life when he introduced him to the Northern Lights junior regional squad. Training became everything.

The Aquatics Centre was a wide boxy cavern of clean concrete and glass; a sterile haven. Alex was often the first person through the changing rooms and onto the poolside. Once stretched, he would take a moment to breathe it all in. The empty audience gallery to his left escarped into the hefty steel rafters. The wall of glass to his right gently steamed by the soft heat of the water, letting in a blaze of low winter sun across the city rooftops. The majestic simplicity of the diving boards at the far end beckoned the sprint. Then came the coil, release and plunge as he shattered the surface and began his daily mile.

Then, winning races became the norm. Winning was everything.

When he turned thirteen, Stanley House started to fall apart because of funding cuts and Vinnie was arrested for something back in his past. Alex never found out what, but he hid behind the blinds of his room and cried as he watched the police take Vinnie away. Alex was rushed through the system to be housed with a new couple, Rosie and Adam. They were religious and had too many ticking clocks in the house for his liking, and lived much further from the Aquatics Centre. But they encouraged his obsession to compete with the same fixated eyes as they gave to their Christian God. In return for their permission and support he behaved himself and went back to school.

And it was there, at Hopford High School, where he began to lose races. He was approaching fourteen and feeling the creaks of change in his body, when the medals of his banner gave way to silver and then to bronze. The gold currency of his talent was giving way to thin brown change.

And he knew the reason why. He only had to look to his fellow racers beside him on the starting blocks to realised why he was falling behind. They had begun to dwarf him; these pubescent giants sprouting hair and muscle mass in all directions whilst he still waited for something to kick-start inside his own body. Inside his sinewy arms, inside his slender legs, inside that still bald thing cringing inside his trunks. In spite of himself, he had trained earlier, breathed deeper, raced harder. But he was failing.

The day he decided to quit was also the day the ocean spoke to him. He had seen hurricanes before, heard their 'tail-ends' howling around outside for days at the end of autumn. He had seen trees snap like wafers and walked through streets that had been turned upside down, but he had never felt one up close. It had amused him how they found such weak names for something that, in its death throes, could pick up a train carriage and hurl it through a building.

Names like Claudette, Dorian, Erin, Fernand.

On the day of the regional qualifiers, held on his home turf, it was Gabrielle who landed. After rising from the Atlantic she ground through Ireland in a matter of hours. Then heading south, they had believed, but she changed her mind and swerved north.

The competition had been underway for an hour when the power started fizzing in and out. Soon, what had started as a gentle breeze outside the wall of glass became a whirling blackness. Falling debris chattered steadily on the roof. The organisers turned up the music to try to hide it; tinny pop music full of shitty cheap vocoders and off-beat bass lines. A wail of uncomforted crying battled against it.

Races were swum to the sound of tentative applause from the packed gallery. Winners were announced by a man and a woman who sounded like they were competing to have the most frantic nervous breakdown. Medals were handed out on scuffed white wooden rostra whereupon the winners would snatch their prizes before retreating to the bunker of the changing rooms. And in the corner, a jury of three sat behind a table hurriedly and nervously tapping notes into laptops as to who they deemed fit for regional selection.

So, when his name was called, Alex raced. He swam his heart out. He scrambled through the water, fired himself from every tumble-turn like a harpoon. He stretched his bones through every stroke, and threw his palm to the tile with predictable results. He lost the 100m freestyle, coming fourth. Then he came an unforgivable fifth in the 50m butterfly. In the group relay, he dropped two places, coming fourth again and so incurred the disgusted glances of his fellow racers to compound his humiliation. He hardly noticed Gabrielle. She could go to hell.

Alex climbed exhausted from the pool, furious with himself. He tore his salt-filled goggles from his face and attacked his pool bag, throwing his towel and blue team jacket inside like rags. He was done. He wanted to claw contemptibly at himself, scratch his skin to ribbons, punch himself. His life was over before it had begun. He wanted to undo his entire wish to ever swim in the first place.

It was Vinnie's fault. Why had he ever encouraged him, if only to fail? He wanted to climb to the highest diving board and hurl his neck at the hard edge of the pool, giving the bastards and their families one final spectacle. He curled his fist tight and looked at the white tile of the wall. Gabrielle raged in his mind.

    'You alright, son?'

He turned to see a coach, dressed in the black and gold of a rival squad, standing beside him.

    'I'm not your fucking son,' he said, and the man backed away.

Alex breathed, and simmered. He uncurled his fist and flexed his hand. Not strong enough, he told himself. You're simply not strong enough. And then he knew who he should hate; his invisible parents and their genetic garbage which he carried. The lazy DNA which refused to change in time for his age, for this race. Then he felt *him* approaching.

His own coach, Carl Knox, bulged through every seam of his blue tracksuit. His was the relaxed, middle-aged muscle of an athletic career that had rested happily, deservedly, on its laurels. Knox's Commonwealth silver medal in 2022 for Freestyle was the pinnacle of a career which Alex would never have. Alex knew instantly what was coming and it wasn't condolence, or encouragement, but one final humiliation.

'Raced well today,' Carl lied with a smile. 'Listen, there's a space in the...'

'I know,' said Alex and thrust his towel into his bag, 'the endurance.'

The underwater swim was normally bolted onto the end of a meeting as something of a novelty, but it was legitimised with the offer of a single medal for the winner. Not all event organisers took it seriously and so not all meetings included it, but it had been appended to the line-up for the benefit and amusement of the jury of three, by whose decisions futures were either being assured or cancelled.

Aside from seeming like a pointless waste of energy, it was also the one race into which any member of a team, regardless of age, could enter. Giants against germs, it was a lottery. Alex knew that his team-mates had each competed in their permitted quota of four races and Alex was available for one more. In the least, they needed a racer to represent the team so as not to incur a team penalty. Obligation got the better of him.

Knox smiled. 'That's the spirit. I knew you wouldn't want to let the others down. We can maintain a bronze lead against the Birmingham lot, which is more than respectable,' Knox added. He flinched as something hard skated across the roof. 'Christ!' he said, looking up then hurried his explanation. 'We just need someone in the water, that's all. You've just got to go through the motions, then we can all go home once Gabrielle's had her fun,' said Knox with a nervous laugh, which Alex took to mean, 'Don't try to win, because you won't. You can't.'

The race was scrambled together in minutes. The gallery had already begun to empty. But Alex could see them through the window of the cafeteria, choking the entrance hall as they waited for a break in the weather to dash to cars. But they were all cut off and Alex found himself grinning at that thought. Let Gabrielle have her fun, he thought. Let this tantrum of the ocean chew the place to bits.

He laughed out loud. Iqbal, the tall boy on the block beside him from the North Yorkshire's, shot him a glance. Alex was the smallest of the racers. The racer on block three was the one who had left him for dead in the freestyle. Alex had learned that he was actually a track and field champion, shunted into the water by his coach as a possible contingency sport. Such a dismissive, easy win mortified Alex, when he compared it with every dawn session in this very pool.

His name boomed over the PA in the line-up and he raised a half-hearted hand to the gallery. He vaguely made out Rosie and Adam wave down but he didn't acknowledge them. When this was over, he would ask to be relocated. Somewhere far away from piss-whipped Manchester and all of its let-downs.

Then, like a switch, it came to him. Standing half-stooped on block six, head up and ready for the launch, stretch and splashdown against his face, he realised, there simply wasn't any point in him being there. To do what? To race against time? To race against the freaks either side of him. This was not a race for time. It was a race for distance. For endurance. He had all the time in the world.

Don't try.

Relief coursed warmly through him. His pulse mellowed. His breathing relaxed. As a consequence, it deepened considerably, just as the chatter of debris on glass to his right seemed to intensify. In amongst Gabrielle's rage, the crack of the gun sounded like a toy.

Calves kicked either side of him and launched into the water. All except his. Instead, he retreated a step from the 'set' position and straightened his back to flex his diaphragm. He pointed his arms upwards and closed his eyes for a moment. He meditated on the deepest breath he could cram into his lungs. He repeated the breath, quicker, then again, faster, then panted, hyperventilating to force his ribs to bend further.

He got a sense of the departing crowds having paused to watch. He pictured Knox's panic and smiled. Then he took in as much air as he could and filled every cell of his body. He opened his eyes, bent his knees, aimed and dived. The water dashed around him in that familiar *thoomsh!* He stretched his arms forward like a spear, undulating his stomach as lithely and calmly as possible. You are a dolphin, he told himself, elegant and effortless. Then he breasted widely through the water.

Ahead he could see the rest of the pack doing the same, with varying degrees of frenetic desperation to catch the lead. He allowed his mind to wander beyond the distorted clatter of the crowd and the pressure creak in his ears.

One racer had quit and bobbed to the surface at two thirds in. Then came the chill blue of the deep end beneath the diving boards. At the bottom lay a single giant vent, only metres away. In a glimmer, he wondered what it would be like to drift down its black throat to the bilges of an underworld. His chest began to burn, his earlier sobs and the chlorine like vinegar in his throat. But before he knew it, he came within touching distance of the wall, of the end.

The lane three giant was already there, bobbing, a hand raised in victory to the gallery. He kicked himself up and out urgently to claim his victory. Others were climbing out too. A clamour of applause reverberated through the water. Four other swimmers burst in succession ahead of him and trod water against the side, exhausted. Alex reached for the wall, the promise of air just inches from him. And now?

He would go through the wall.

Alex pulled his arm away. He threw his body down and curled into the tumble. He pitched his body into a corkscrew to reverse direction and coiled his legs tight against the side. He turned left to catch a glimpse of Iqbal who had submerged his face to look at him. Iqbal beckoned him up urgently. Alex grinned and gave him his middle finger.

No.

Alex sprang from the tiles. He threw his arms forward into the sharpest point he could muster and forced his contracted stomach to flow as he rippled into a series of quick butterfly kicks.

But the oxygen was gone, only a stagnant pressure in his mouth. He gritted his teeth so hard that his jaw muscles burned. Blood filled his forehead. Plus ten metres... A thundering vibration filled his ears. As stars began to sing and burst in his vision, he knew the nature of the noise. It was the stamping, the cheering of the crowd. All eyes were on him, he realised. They could see the stunt he was pulling and they loved him for it.

Plus fifteen metres...

He pulled and pulled, breast-stroking as widely as possible,

cupping his hands to grip the water. He left the harsh chill of the deep end and his body instinctively seemed to pull him to the surface. The need to breathe had become a rage inside him and his body's natural buoyancy wanted to carry him back to air. He resisted, stroking deeper to compensate.
No.
You are not swimming horizontally, he told himself. You are swimming upwards through ocean. You are in a sinking ship and you are the last one to pull free from the suction that has killed everyone around you. You are a thousand spirits clambering from the traps and locks that drowned them. You are escaping from the bilges of the world.
Ten metres to go...
You have no choice but to kick or to drown. You have no time and you are at depth. You are a stranded diver. You are winning and they are roaring.
The cheering enveloped him with its electricity. Five metres to go. The world seemed to flicker. He blinked, bit down hard. Then the water went inky grey. Another blackout. The water fragmented in his vision, crystalline shapes falling, pirouetting.
Shards of glass.
Something plunged off to his right and he jerked. Something angular. Bubbles floated away and it came into focus.
A pushchair, its buckles and harness adrift. Then something crashed behind him. He felt the concussion of it break the water and thrust him forwards. As he turned his head to look, something else plunged off to his left; the twisted red triangle of a car door.
His outstretched fingers crumpled into the side with a jagged pain. He burst from the water and the world roared. Air punched his ear drums. He clamped his hands to the side of his head. He fought to swallow great, desperate lungfuls of air as his mouth filled with whirling grit. It dashed his face, snatched for his eyes. He looked to the empty balcony. Rows of seats rippled and were torn away in shreds. He was alone.
A piece from one of the springboards cartwheeled past his head. The wall of glass was now a buckled aluminium grid, every pane shattered. The frames flexed under the weight of a red car jammed into it thirty feet up. The only light in the world came from four orange hazard lights blinking plaintively as the

world rioted through the gaps.

The pool was being dashed with branches, posts, pieces of sharp colour as though it were magnetised. The surface of the water itself was being blasted in a curve against the opposite side as though trying to slither over the lip and cower in the drains.

The roof buckled upwards once, then twice, then folded back like foil, as if hoisted by a chain somewhere in the stratosphere. Black water raged upon him then Alex felt himself jolt upwards. He shielded his face awaiting the pull of the storm, the vacuum to the end. Then he felt himself bend and flop down over someone's shoulder.

He saw black and gold on the person's trousers. There was blood coming from somewhere. His or theirs, he could not tell. He was wrangled through a doorway, into safety and shadow. The last thing he saw of his pool were the three white cubes of the rostra blur through the air and dash to splinters against the wall.

August Morning
I Robin Irie

August 01, 1838
Pindars Valley Plantation, Clarendon Parish, Jamaica, British West Indies

Gussie tried to focus on the dominoes on the table in front of him. There was so much going through his mind. He looked east, into the dark sky. It seemed to be getting lighter but maybe his mind was playing tricks on him.

'Play yu card, man,' said Niney, who sat to Gussie's right, 'or say yu pass if yu pass.'

Gussie looked at Niney who held his three remaining dominoes in his left hand that was missing a forefinger. Niney grinned at Gussie but his eyes looked shifty in the torch light.

'Make haste and come to mi,' said Niney.

Gussie ignored Niney's bluff and studied the game, trying to recall who hadplayed what. It came back to him. His partner, Step Twelve, who sat opposite him had played the three, and Yellowman who sat to his left, the five. He looked at the dominoes in his hand; five-three, double-three, and three-blank. He looked up at Step Twelve who leaned forward and said, 'pass di boy and come!'

In a game of dominoes, a player was not allowed to tell his partner how to play or what dominoes he held, but Step

Twelve's action was as close as it got. Gussie slammed down his five-three, hitting the five and making both ends three.

'Aye!' said Step Twelve, slapping his thigh in mock pain.

'Your play,' said Gussie to Niney.

'Where him going to find play from?' asked Step Twelve.

Niney tapped the table indicating that he was taking a pass.

'Mi tell yu dat little boy no belong in big man tings,' said Step Twelve, slamming down his four-three so hard that the dominoes jumped up on the table.

'Play yu one card and go to mi pardner,' he said to Yellowman, who looked at his partner before pushing back the dominoes that had jumped out of line.

'How much yu have?' Yellowman asked Niney.

'Three,' said Niney. His voice betrayed nothing.

'How much yu have, Gussie?'

Gussie put his dominoes down and removed his hand to show two.

Yellowman played four-blank, and Gussie turned his dominoes over showing his winning hand; three-blank and double-three.

'Play one,' said Niney, reaching for his bamboo cup and taking a drink of his rum. They had drunk so much rum all night that Gussie had gone nose-blind to the pungent smell.

'Yu serious, man?' asked Step Twelve. 'Den yu expect di man going to kill him double-three?'

'Make him play,' insisted Niney.

Gussie played three-blank, hitting the blank and turning to the game three at both ends. As there were no other threes apart from his double-three the game was over.

'Four love!' declared Step Twelve, throwing in his hand. A round of dominoes goes on until one team wins six games. Niney's team hadn't won any so far so it was four love. They all threw in their hands.

'Loser's shuffle,' said Gussie, picking up his own cup of rum from under the table as he watched Step Twelve limp away to piss against a bush. It was said that he extended his bad leg twelve and drew back six for each step, hence his nickname Step Twelve And Draw Back Six. That was too much of a mouthful, so now it was simply Step Twelve.

With a start, Gussie realised that he should not have been able to see Step Twelve against the bush, not in proper darkness. He blinked and looked into his rum, daylight was coming. A ball welled up inside his stomach, a ball of pure joy. Gussie looked around the yard where other men and women played dominoes or just sat chatting in small groups. Did they feel it too? They must do, he concluded.

Niney had finished shuffling the dominoes and they selected their hand of seven dominoes each. Step Twelve would have to take what was left. Gussie drank some more rum to settle his nerves and looked at the sky again. Step Twelve returned and took his seat as someone else walked over to their table. Gussie did not need the lamplight to know that it was Noseworthy, because you saw that prominent nose before you saw him, or so the saying went.

'Boy, Gussie, the way yu beating dat rum, yu better pray dat full freedom really come through or dog nyam yu supper,' said Noseworthy.

Gussie looked up at him. Pray? Black people have been doing nothing but pray for the last two hundred years since backra maasa brought them to this land. No, he was done praying, and there would be fire and blood if full freedom didn't come with the morning.

'Freedom will come,' said Yellowman. His voice carried no doubt.

'How can yu be so sure?' asked Noseworthy, leaning against a tree and rolling a cigarette.

'Dat's what mi father said.'

'What yu father know?' asked Noseworthy.

'Not him, mi real father,' said Yellowman. Like many slaves with his colour, his real father was one of the overseers. That was why he was chosen for the Great House, even though he preferred to spend his free time with the field slaves.

Gussie tried not to think too much of what was being said. He didn't want to think at all. 'Yu want mi to pose?' he asked Step Twelve.

'Yeah man, gwaan,' said Step Twelve.

'Mi no know,' said Noseworthy. He sighed loudly. 'Is not the first time dem say wi getting full freedom and it no come through. Mi will wait till daylight and see.'

Gussie looked at the dominoes in his hand; five pieces of aces. He played five-ace; a sporting pose, and Step Twelve sat up straight. Niney tapped the table to take a pass and everyone looked at him.

'Mi pardner!' said Step Twelve, 'Yu stay good, man,' he paused and studied his hand before playing a six-five.

'Mi will believe it when mi see it,' said Noseworthy.
Step Twelve rounded on him. 'What happen to yu, man? What make yu so curmudgeon? Eh? Yu just want to drag down everybody's mood tonight?'

'Yu can stay there,' insisted Noseworthy. 'Mi older than all of yu, and mi know how dem backra wicked.'

'Cool yuself,' said Niney. 'Parson say it going to happen.'

'Parson say, Parson say,' said Noseworthy. He hissed through his teeth. 'Parson say, but him is just a man. What yu say?'

'Yu mustn't say tings like dat about a man of God,' said Niney.
Gussie felt a hand on his shoulder and looked up to see Millie. His wife had one hand resting protectively on her bulging belly. A thought made Gussie shiver. She couldn't be ready yet. A cold feeling washed over him.

'Yu mother wake up,' she said. 'She want yu.'
Gussie breathed a sigh of relief and got to his feet. He was tempted to touch Millie's belly, but no, not here. He smiled at the thought. 'Mama want mi,' he said to the table. 'Millie will play mi hand.'

'Woii!' said Step Twelve to the others. 'Disgrace wi going to disgrace yu now dat belly-woman going to beat yu.'
Gussie held the chair steady for Millie to sit then went to see his mother. There was a shuffling from the chickens in the orange tree as he passed. Yes, daylight was not far off. He swallowed the lump in his throat. Freedom, full freedom; the thought made his head spin.

'Mama?' he said entering her room. The place stank of sickness.

'Gussie?' her voice was weak. 'Come sit down beside mi.'
He went over and sat on the edge of the bed and took her hand

into his. It twitched as if she was trying to squeeze his hand but lacked the strength. Mama was sick, very sick, and it was a miracle that she was still alive.

'Daylight yet?' asked Mama.

Gussie leaned to look through the door. Yes, dawn was definitely here. 'Soon Mama, not long from now.'

She released a long breath and for a while there was just silence.

'Mi want yu to do something for mi,' said Mama

'Of course, Mama, anything yu say.'

'Mi want yu to find yu father.'

He looked at Mama in the poor light. His father was five years dead. Was her mind going? 'Mama, Papa dead long time.'

'No,' said Mama. 'Dolphus was not yu real father. Him get with mi when mi was already with yu.'

Gussie felt hot all over. Could this be true? His father was not his father. Anger rose inside him but guttered when he looked at Mama's frail body. How could he be angry at her? 'What yu saying to mi, Mama?'

Her eyes opened to look at him and snapped back shut. 'Mi was a pretty girl when mi was young,' her voice was shaky but carried an edge of pride. 'All kind of men wanted mi, but it was Georgie dat catch mi eye.'

Gussie could have sworn that a smile passed over her face.

'Georgie did tall and handsome, just like yu - people say dat yu is a dead stamp of him.' She stopped speaking and breathed heavily.

Gussie didn't know how to feel. A part of him felt betrayed, like his whole life was a lie, but another part of him wanted to know more about this man with whom he shared blood; the man who gave him his looks. He did not press Mama. He waited.

'Mi wish mi did have more time to tell yu everything; but one day mi was packing sugarcane on the cart and it look like the rope pop and the whole ting tumble down. Di driver start to beat mi bad across mi back with him whip and mi drop on di ground and was bawling. Georgie hear mi and run over and grab di whip from di driver and cut him two lash with it before dem hold him down.'

She paused to catch her breath again and Gussie felt his hatred for the backras grow. The parson always talked about the devil and hell, but if there is really a hell, it must be on the plantation and the white man must be the devil. How could hell be any worse?

'Dem tie him up on a tree and when dem done with him, not a spot no left on him back dat whip no touch. Di next day, dem sell him off because him too hard to control.' Despite the weak monotone, Gussie could hear the sadness and loss that tinged her voice.

'Is after dat mi find out dat mi was with yu. Dolphus start court mi and him never mind dat mi was with another man's child, so wi married and him treat yu like him own. Him was a good man but him was never mi Georgie. Mi always ask about him and di last ting mi hear, him was on a coffee plantation in St John parish.'

She stopped and caught her breath again. This time it took longer for her breathing to settle down.

'Dolphus was a good, good man and him was all di father yu ever need, but yu blood is yu blood. Is what connect yu back with the old spirit dem. A man must always know where him come from.'

Her voice died away and the chatter outside seemed louder in the ensuing silence. Gussie looked at mama, his mind racing as it tried to make sense of what she had told him. She laid so still that he had to put his hand to her nose to make sure that she was still breathing. He held her hand thinking; so much to think about. Gussie sat like that until the crowing of the rooster intruded on his thoughts. Daylight! Gussie almost jumped up. Gently, he rested Mama's hand on the bed and walked to the doorway. The rooster crowed again and was soon answered by another, and then another.

Gussie went back inside and knelt beside Mama's bed. He took her hand in both of his. 'Mama?'

Mama took a sharp intake of breath, 'Hhmm?'

'Daylight, Mama.'

'Daylight?' she repeated.

'Yes, Mama, daylight.'

Mama breathed in and out weakly. 'And no driver no come calling out?'

Gussie listened. 'No, Mama.'

'Good,' she said, 'dat is very good.'

Gussie felt tears welling up in his eyes. He leaned forward and kissed Mama on the cheeks.

'Yes, Mama. It really good.'

'Yes,' she said. 'Go to yu wife now, Gussie. And remember to tell the children dat dem grandmother never dead as no slave.'

Gussie wiped his eyes, he could no longer hold back the tears. He kissed Mama again and got up. When he got back outside the domino games were paused as the table tops were being pounded like drums. Some people danced around and clapped while others sat looking dazed with faces turned in the direction of the Great House.

His eyes sought out Millie. She was sitting on the chair looking at him with the biggest smile splitting her face. He ran to her. 'Wi free!' he blurted out. 'Millie, wi free,' he said through laughter and tears.

Millie stretched out a hand to him and he took it, going down on his knees.

'Wi free,' he told her belly. He kissed her belly and was sure he felt the child move inside her.

'Wi free!' he told it, 'and yu will never be born as a slave.'

ABOUT THE AUTHORS

Janet Inglis is a retired teacher. She was born in Scotland, grew up in Liverpool, and, apart for a short time teaching in Africa, has lived the rest of her life in Birmingham. She now lives with her husband near Cannon Hill park. There have been phases in her life where she has been obsessed by writing stories. Her retirement has been one long phase of writing mania. Only this time she wants people to read her stories.

Kathryn Cooper has recently completed the first draft of a novel, a new genre for her. She has been writing radio plays for several years and received positive feedback for two of them, both getting to the second stage of the BBC Writer's Room selection process, but not actually being commissioned. She has also written a screenplay, short stories and flash fiction. One of her short stories came second place in a University of Birmingham Creative Writing anthology competition, and she was shortlisted for the Bridport Prize in 2016 for flash fiction. 'Morta' was inspired by a visit to Rome.

Evelyn 'Evie' Kemp is a mid-30 something year old, who has been writing almost her whole life. She has had poems published while she was at school. She writes an array of genres spanning from dystopian fiction, to horror and sci-fi and general fiction documenting everyday life. As a proud self-proclaimed nerd, she has a love for history, the unusual and is an avid reader. She currently lives in Birmingham with a menagerie of animals and her biggest fan, her partner.

Andrew Brazier spent fifteen years as an actor before studying theology and entering ministry in the Methodist Church. On a path that took him from stand-up comedy to writing alternative liturgy for same sex marriage and the LGBTQ community, the key factor was the rhythm of language. Whilst still very much wearing his L plates in terms of short stories and novels, Andrew has a background in script writing for theatre. A reviewer once noted, 'he had no idea where the writer was taking him, but the view was lovely on the way.'

Sarah Bartlett runs a successful freelance copywriting business from her home in Birmingham. Creative writing gives her the freedom to explore broader themes and questions in fictional form. She particularly enjoys writing about the intersection of politics in personal life. In other writings, ghosts make frequent appearances. Sarah keeps an open mind on the paranormal but is interested in the psychology of the haunted, living individual. Originally from Manchester, Sarah also enjoys swimming and foreign languages, and plays the clarinet.

S. L. Jones is a social-casual writer, salsa dancer and Careers Adviser in Birmingham and has been a member of Moseley Writing Group since 2017 and a member of Birmingham Writing Group (BWG) from slightly earlier in the same year and can highly recommend them. He wonder if one might learn as much from a writing group as they can with an MA, it's a lot cheaper! He feels his writing ability has tripled since joining. He is three quarters through a historical fiction novel set 1680-1780, a third through a Sci Fi Novella and a quarter through another historical set 1899-1917. This will be his third published work after submissions to BWG's *City of Hope* and *City of Night.*

Sofia Kokolaki-Hall is an Athenian, a scouser and a brummie. She drinks out of a martini glass, even if she's drinking tap water. She's written flash fiction, short stories and poems, and her first novel *The Fearless Existence of Pandora Jones* is ready to pop.

Lucy Smallbone lives in Birmingham with her husband, three children, five fish and two guinea pigs. After several years as a primary school teacher, she took a career break and now has the pleasure of writing in her free time. When she's not writing, she can be found painting, cycling, tap dancing, singing and performing. She has written lyrics for songs performed live, enjoys writing children's verse, short stories and in the process of writing a YA novel. One of her proudest moments was achieving Grade 5 in Music Theatre at 41 years of age.

David Croser grew up in the far north of England in the Border country. As well as being the author of *Rice Pudding Reality*, an anthology of his early stories, he is author of *A Foretaste of Infinity*, an anthology of his London stories. He is the editor of *City of Night*, an anthology of stories from the Birmingham Writers Group, and their second anthology *City of Hope.* He has also contributed stories to a number of other anthologies. He lives in Solihull with his hubby and three cats. One of these days he might actually finish a full-length novel.

P V Mroso, son of a farmer, was born on the slopes of Mount Kilimanjaro and came to UK to study. Currently he is a retired Pharmacist who spends his time writing folk stories, and growing fruits and vegetables. The taste of fresh garden fruits, the making of jam and wine has become the motivation to carry on.

Faith Walsh was born in Birmingham and lives in Moseley. She likes writing, meeting up with friends, travelling, Italy, reading, ancient history, trying different ice cream flavours, eating curries, going to the theatre and ballet, meals out, visiting museums, sitting in cafes, walking in parks, visiting art galleries, yoga, trying to make myself understood in another language, meandering, and pottering.

Sarah Aust was born in Birmingham and has lived there most of her life apart from university in York and six months in South Wales. She works as a nurse and has been working on a novel for what seems like half her life.

S W Mackman lives in Birmingham with a daughter, a hamster, and a small potted plant.

T.B. Donne has been writing for thirty years. During the first twenty-seven they finished three short stories. Since joining Moseley Writers, they have finished six more. Moseley Writers is great.

Chris Randall is Creative Director of Second Home Studios, an animation company based in the shadow of a Digbeth railway arch in Birmingham since 2004. The studio creates work in all styles of animation, from serious to silly, with a reputation for striking stop-motion work. The portfolio features BAFTA, RTS and British Animation Award winning films, and also includes work in related crafts such as visual effects and traditional puppetry. Chris writes predominantly in the science-fiction genre. He also produced a really nifty cover for this anthology.

I Robin Irie grew up in Jamaica and writes stories that draw on this rich culture. His interest in history causes him to mine the past for inspiration. He is currently seeking an agent for his first novel; an epic fantasy with an African setting. A husband and a father, he spends his days masquerading as an accountant, which is totally congruous with being a writer of fiction. He is also a long-suffering fan of Arsenal Football Club.

Printed in Great Britain
by Amazon